BEERS AND FEARS:
THE HAUNTED BREWERY

CHUCK BUDA, FRANK EDLER, TIM MEYER, & ARMAND ROSAMILIA

EVIL EPOCH
PRESS

BEERS AND FEARS:
THE HAUNTED BREWERY

Published by Evil Epoch Press

Cover design by Najla Qamber Designs

Images:

Copyright © Shutterstock/Sam72

Copyright © istock/nwbob

International Standard Book Number (ISBN):
978-1-7323993-2-7

Printed in the United States of America

BEERS AND FEARS:
THE HAUNTED BREWERY

THE LAST TAPROOM ON THE EDGE OF THE WORLD

(1)

AS LIGHTNING BEGAN to crash around the small dive attached to the Ocean View Hotel, Paul McDaniel found a cozy spot in the corner all to himself. It wasn't difficult. Like most nights, the bar was lacking foot traffic. A few of the hotel's customers drifted in and out, looking for cheap beer specials and shit bar food, but fled immediately once they saw the beers on tap. Double IPAs and copper-colored saisons. Chocolate coffee stouts and coconut ales. But no light beer. Not in Paul McDaniel's place.

He sipped slowly from his dark brown porter, enjoying the cool, refreshing taste that filled his mouth. As he mused over what renovations he should complete by next summer—brighten the décor, replace the knotty pine paneling with tile and drywall, hang some hipster art, give the place a contemporary look and abandon that God-awful 70s touch—the alarm on his cell phone sounded, alerting him that he had an appointment in five minutes, one he'd almost entirely forgotten.

The writer.

Last week, he'd received a call from Lance Nolan, a writer from New York who specialized in real-life haunted house stories, tales of the supernatural and all that wonderful spooky stuff that was so damn popular nowadays. Nolan was pretty well-known around these parts, as most of his story material came from the tri-state area, but the rest of the world had hardly heard of him. He'd published three books to date, all on famous hauntings, and he'd been a guest on a few of those television specials; ones that recounted ghost stories and had titles like "My Wife, The Demon" or "An Invader Took My Daughter to Hell." The kind with terrible actors and actresses playing the parts of *real* people.

Paul didn't think much of Nolan's writing, had hardly gotten through his first published piece and had never bothered with the other two, but he'd seemed nice enough on the phone. Sincere. Easy to talk to. A genuinely good guy who just wanted to tell a story.

Of course, he had, Paul told himself. *He just wants your stories. All the good stuff. Every strange tale.*

Thunder roared overhead, rattling the table, the walls, and the glassware behind the bar. Sylvester, the underpaid bartender from Romania, ducked when the god-like roar boomed over them.

Paul snorted. "Easy there, hotshot. It's just a little storm."

The local weatherman had predicted a few short showers but nothing more. Paul was surprised to hear the torrential downpour slapping against the outside patio so furiously. Normally, he'd enjoy the evening out on the deck, looking across the beach and into the calm black ocean waters. But not tonight.

Tonight, the sky had fallen on Ocean View, New Jersey.

"I no like thunder," Sylvester stated, returning to his duty of hand-washing the empty beer mugs. "Bad omen when it thunders like that."

The lights flickered in response.

Paul waved his hand in the air and smiled. "Go back to work, you superstitious fuck."

The bartender did as he was told, indifferent to Paul's vulgarity. After all, Paul had called him worse. Hateful things he only said when he was angry and when business was slow, which was often now that the small breweries were taking over, popping up on every street corner and gobbling up his share of the market.

Sylvester and the other bartenders weren't responsible for Paul's business woes, but he sure liked to blame them. *You're not smiling enough,* he'd tell them. *No one wants their drinks served by a statue. Talk to the people! Have a conversation! Jesus, have you never worked in customer service?*

Now that he thought about it, he had been a little rough on his employees over the years. He paid them spit and often talked down to them—not the kind of leader his father had raised.

"Sylvester," Paul said, his voice tranquil. He cocked his head back and threw the rest of the beer down his gullet. He wiped away a foamy mustache with his wrist and raised his empty glass in the air. "Bring me another, please."

Sylvester hustled to the tap, poured a new glass, and brought over the refill at once.

"Thank you kindly. Sylvester, have I told you how much I appreciate your work ethic?"

Sylvester's bright blue eyes darted back and forth. Lightning flashed in the windows. Thunder rolled like the growl of some cosmic horror. "Sir?"

"You know, I just wanted to say, that I, uh..." This was much harder than he had envisioned. "Well, you do a good job and I just wanted to let you know. No big deal or anything."

Sylvester nodded and kept his mouth closed. He returned to the bar and continued his nightly routine.

"Jesus," Paul said, sipping his beer. "Can't even give a guy a compliment nowadays."

As he looked down at his books, the sad numbers from the previous week looking slightly out of focus, two things happened, almost at once: firstly, a deafening boom of thunder shook the hotel bar, sounding much louder and closer than the first rumble. The noise was so forceful that two mugs fell off the shelf behind the bar and shattered on the floor next to Sylvester. The barkeep looked over at his boss, his skin noticeably losing its color. Before Paul could open his mouth and scold the tall, lanky bastard for keeping the glassware so close to the edge of the shelf, thing number two happened: the writer had entered the bar, pushing his wet mane of hair back, off his face.

Great, Paul thought to himself, *this is really happening.* A part of him had wished the hack had never shown. Not like he had anything better going on, but this would be a complete waste of time. No one would believe the stories about that place, that brewery set on the edge of the world. The edge of time.

The edge of Hell.

"Good evening," the man said, his voice small, barely audible over the rainfall.

"Heya, sport," Paul said, not bothering to rise to greet him.

The writer took off his raincoat and hung it on the hook next to the door. "Sorry I'm late. The storm is getting out of control."

"No worries. Sylvester and I were just enjoying each other's company." He nodded at the tall man. "Isn't that right, old friend?"

Sylvester didn't reply and continued to sweep up the broken glass.

Paul shrugged. "Eh. Why don't you have a seat."

Lance Nolan, notebook tucked under his arm, made his way across the bar and took the seat opposite of Paul. "Thank you for meeting with me. I really appreciate it."

Paul nodded, giving the man a once over. *Man?* he thought to himself. *Hell, he's practically a kid.* He looked to be about thirty, a guess that Paul was willing to wager next month's profits on. He had long dark hair that was pulled back in a ponytail, colorful tattoos down both arms, and glasses that sat perfectly on his face. He didn't look like a writer, but, then again, Paul didn't really know what writers were supposed to look like. He had a preconceived notion that all male writers dressed in argyle sweaters and khakis, kept their short hair combed neatly back, and had noticeable symptoms of scoliosis from sitting in a chair and typing all day long.

"You look a bit young to be a writer," Paul said. "I mean, no offense."

"None taken," Nolan said, getting himself situated. He opened his notebook to a blank page and set down his pen next to it. Pulling a tape recorder out of his breast pocket, the writer arched his brow. "Mind if I record?"

Paul smiled. "Not at all."

"Thank you." He put the recorder down next to the other items. The last thing he retrieved was a pocket-sized tin of home-rolled cigarettes. "Mind if I smoke?"

Paul shook his head. "Not at all. *Mi casa, es su casa.*"

"Appreciate it. It was a long drive and I don't like to smoke with the windows up." He lit his black cigarette and shifted in his seat, trying to get comfortable. After he found his sweet spot, he rested his elbows on the table and stared directly at Paul. "So, first of all, thanks for taking the time to meet with me. Most people would disregard me as some sort of nutjob and hang up on me the second they heard my pitch."

"What can I say? I like to help when I can."

"Let's get right into it then."

"Sure."

"I'm here to talk about Bayberry Bluff."

Hearing the name spoken aloud, one he hadn't heard in many, many years, sent a sharp chill down his back. "Ah. *That* place." He stared beyond Nolan, somewhere into the past. There were so many stories, so many strange tales. He didn't know where Nolan wanted to start, and he couldn't even think of a logical place *to* start. "Sorry. Haven't actually spoken about Bayberry in quite some time. It's weird even hearing the name out loud."

"I think it's safe to say the place has gone through some interesting iterations over the years. Wouldn't you say?"

"Oh yes," he said fondly. "Very interesting. Everything from an abandoned insane asylum to, most recently, over the past thirty-something years, a marginally successful local brewing company. Some tasty ales have come out of that place, that's for sure."

Along with other things, he wanted to say, but refrained.

"Before we get into it, tell me a little about yourself. How do you fit into the legend of Bayberry Bluff?"

A forced chuckle escaped Paul's lips. "How do I fit in? Well, my father was a local brewmaster in these parts for almost forty years before he passed almost a decade ago. He'd worked at Bayberry Bluff when the first brewery opened—that's where he started, where he perfected his craft. I worked there, too, in the eighties, off and on, during a low period when the two of us weren't speaking."

"Hm," Paul said, jotting down notes. "Did you learn how to brew in that place?"

"I learned mostly from my old man, but he learned at Bayberry, so in a way—yeah, yeah, I did."

"Interesting."

Paul didn't think it was all that interesting; the interesting stuff came later. *The stories. The horrifying truths of that place.*

"You didn't come here to talk about that, though. Did you, Mr. Nolan?"

Nolan froze, then settled back in his chair. "No, no, I did not."

"You came to talk about the spooky shit that goes on in that place. That *went* on there. The hauntings. The weird, unexplainable occurrences. The tall tales and local legends. After all, you're not writing a book on local craft beer or the sudden popularity of home-brewing. Are you?"

Nolan's silence was answer enough.

"I'll tell you what you came to hear. I have enough stories about that place to help fill your book—some things I've witnessed, some I've gathered from credible sources."

"Thought I'd get to know the storyteller a bit." He tapped his notebook with the pen. "For the story."

"People won't care about me. I'm just an old man who's spent his entire life making beer. That's not why people will pick up your book. They'll pick up your book because the events that have taken place at Bayberry Bluff over the years will haunt them forever. The tales that have come from that place will infect their dreams, like a virus. They'll read your book because Bayberry Bluff is a place of evil. A site of sin. It's a place that doesn't quite exist in the same reality as the one we reside in."

Nolan swallowed. "So, you're saying the local legends are true?"

The old brewmaster smiled. "I'm only telling you my opinion, Mr. Nolan. I guess you'll have to judge for yourself."

"Before we get started, I want your honest assessment—as someone who's been there, worked there, and has lived within twenty miles of the place all his life—plain and simple—is Bayberry Bluff exactly what people paint it to be? A haunted place? A place where demons dwell? There are some people on the Internet who claim Bayberry Bluff is actually a gateway to Hell. What do you say to that?"

Paul's lips curled near the edges. "They are all wrong." Then, casually, he shrugged. "And they're all right."

Just then, lightning sparked the skies, brightening the room. The power surged again but stayed on. Thunder crashed all around them, shaking the world with its fury.

Sylvester cowered behind the bar again, ducking as if someone had chucked a bottle at his head.

"That was timely," Nolan said, smirking.

Paul wondered if he'd still be smirking after the first story. He wondered if the young man's mind could handle more than one tale. He wondered how many it would take for him to believe. Or if he was the kind of guy who required proof—actual proof—that these things existed.

By night's end, he would know.

"Some say," Paul said, running his finger along the edge of his glass, "that Bayberry Bluff was built on top of an ancient Indian burial ground." He yawned. "Possible, I guess, but oh-so cliché. Others will have you believe that the place was once a brothel, owned by a witch in the late 1700s, that she placed a hex on the place, cursing all of her customers and everyone who ever stepped foot on her property." Another non-caring twitch of his shoulders. "Not sure I'm on board with that one."

"What else do they say about it?" Nolan asked, leaning forward. "I mean, the only thing I can confirm is that it was an asylum in the early 1900s, a place for the criminally insane, and that it closed and reopened several times over the years and closed permanently in the early 1960s." He licked his dry lips, nearly drooling over the legend of Bayberry Bluff. "I'd like to know more. I'd like to know everything. And I think you're the person who can do that, Mr. McDaniel."

The storyteller is hooked, Paul thought to himself. *Let him in. Give him the secrets. Let him tell the story of Bayberry Bluff.*

Maybe the world needs to know the truth.

"Some agree that Bayberry Bluff doesn't actually exist in our world. Some say it sits on the outskirts of Hell, a mystical place that resides between our world and the one veiled in shadows, where dark, dangerous things lurk. They say it's a place where anything can happen, and anything does."

Nolan paused so he could find his voice. "Is... is that what you believe, Mr. McDaniel?"

"Doesn't matter what I believe."

"Will you tell me the stories of that place? What you've seen? What you've heard?"

Paul considered it a moment, as if dragging the kid into this mess was still up for debate. It wasn't too late to stop this, but, once he started, there was no going back. He wouldn't be able to take back what was said, the stories; they'd be a part of him, as they had always been a part of Paul.

They need to be told, urged a voice, surely not his own. *It's time to tell the truth of what goes on there.*

"Will you?" Nolan asked again, eager to hear the horrors. Suddenly, the thirty-ish man was just a young boy begging an old man to tell him one more story before bedtime. "Please tell me. I've traveled all this way."

Paul nodded slowly. "I'll tell you. I'll tell you stories, *three* of them. Three I believe to be the truest of any of the tales that have come out of that place."

Gripping his pen, Nolan nodded. He was ready.

Or was he?

Paul didn't know.

"But to tell the tales, we'll first need beer." He signaled

14

Sylvester to bring over another round. "Lots and lots of beer."

Outside, lightning streaked across the cloud-cluttered sky. Thunder clapped. The rain continued to assault the small New Jersey town.

Outside, something sinister braved the storm.

NO FORTUNATE SON

BLAZE SLAMMED DOWN the keg. The ancient wood floor creaked under the heft of the beer. Brushing his calloused hands together, he scanned the brewery, worried his boss would catch a glimpse of the two men who stood in the doorway.

Dougie and a slick-haired clown in a bourbon-colored leisure suit.

The fading sunlight glowed around the shadowed shapes entering the brewery. Blaze nodded at the pair, signaling them to follow him. He stared at his scuffed boots as he made his way across the bar to the door marked for employees only.

As the men slipped inside, Blaze closed the door behind him before they were noticed.

"Why are you here?" Blaze asked Dougie, while he eyed the man in the suit. Cockiness dripped off the man's haughty sneer. His face showed a dark shadow of whiskers, which crept up to the thick graying sideburns. Blaze ran a hand through his dark hair. It still felt strange to have his hair back, after living with a crew cut for the past several years.

"It's time we had a chat." Dougie fidgeted with the tassels dangling from his rawhide leather jacket. Blaze knew Dougie was a bona fide hippie with his long hair and tie-dyed outfits. But Dougie looked like an Indian chief, leather moccasins matching the jacket.

"What about?" Blaze paused to listen at the door, afraid his boss would stumble upon them. "I'm at work, you know?"

Dougie chuckled. He glanced at his companion, rubbing the faint blonde beard on his chin. "Hey man, business is business. You're late on your payment."

Blaze stiffened. He began to work through his next steps. First, he would strike the greaseball in the throat to incapacitate him. Then he would bring the fight to Dougie. Blaze wouldn't allow them to beat him up easily. Not that he was too concerned. He was thicker than both men and believed he could out strike them if it came to blows.

ARE YOU CRAZY? IT'S MAFIA. THEY'LL KILL YOU.

Blaze shifted slightly to the left in order to make his body a smaller target.

"I'm sorry. I had to pay rent this week so I'm short. You know I'm good for it. Have I ever screwed you before?" Blaze turned his attention to the man in the suit. "What's he gonna do? Beat me?"

The greaseball grimaced and moved in Blaze's direction as if to prove his toughness. Dougie stretched his arm across the man's chest to keep him in place. "Blaze. Don't be stupid. Tony is only here to talk." Tony cracked his knuckles and smirked at Blaze. "That's all. Nobody is hitting anybody. Okay?"

Blaze steeled himself for a sucker punch. He didn't believe Dougie. Not that Dougie had ever lied to him in the past. But a drug dealer was a drug dealer. Even if that drug dealer looked like a cheap imitation of John Lennon.

Dougie stepped closer to Blaze. He slowly perched his scrawny arm around Blaze's shoulder. Blaze allowed the friendly gesture, but he prepared for what might come next. Dougie walked Blaze across the storeroom. The smell of stale beer and dust permeated the cases of liquor and spare tables. Blaze strained his ears to keep tabs on any sudden movements from where Tony remained.

"Look, I like you Blaze. I really do. But you gotta understand, I have mouths to feed. And those mouths have a lot of power." Dougie glanced behind Blaze at Tony. He lowered his voice. "These guys don't like to be stiffed. I'd cover for you myself, you know I would. But I just don't have the means right now."

Blaze wiggled free of Dougie's arm. He glared at Tony. Tony chewed a stick of bubble gum as he grinned at Blaze. "So, what's there to talk about? You guys are gonna break my legs and then leave."

Dougie laughed. He got Tony to join in the mirth. Dougie swung his long hair over his shoulder with one hand. "I told you. Nobody is breaking nothing. We might be able to come to another arrangement."

Blaze scratched his dark scalp. He bristled at the offer he knew was coming. Because he had been in Vietnam and had done lots of killing, they would task him with knocking off some other mob boss in order to pay his debts. The job would end up getting him killed anyway. A whole army of greaseballs would stand between him and the target. His chances would be minimal. And these guys wouldn't care because Blaze couldn't be tied back to The Family.

Tony approached, his shiny dress shoes scuffing the dirty floor. The smell of Tony's cheap cologne nauseated Blaze. His bubblegum snapped. Black eyes looked back at Blaze, crowned by smiling laugh lines.

"This is a good deal, Blake."

"It's Blaze."

"Whatever. This country is great because of guys like you. My own Pop fought in France. Killed lots of Krauts. Suffered many tragedies. Came back here and gave my brothers and sisters a good life." Tony circled Blaze as he spoke. "The things he seen over there, it was rough. I'm sure you seen things too, huh?"

Blaze folded his arms. Dougie winked at him, acknowledging his impatience with the deal. He rolled his eyes. Tony paused, scanning the chaos of the inventory in the storeroom.

"Bad things make you appreciate the good times. You kill a bunch of chinks. And what has your country done for you? Squat. You're not welcome anywhere. Got no friends. Family don't want to be seen with you. And now you're hooked. I feel for you."

"Is there a point to this? My boss is gonna lose his shit

19

if he finds us back here." Blaze stepped toward the door. He restrained himself from peeking into the bar. Blaze didn't want to blow his one opportunity to hold down a steady job.

Tony put his hands on his hips, his jacket flapped over his arms. The powder blue shirt cuffs rode up to reveal an expensive gold watch and fingers full of rings. "You have to take advantage, Blake. We can become...partners." Tony opened his arms as if to invite Blaze into his life. "One hand washes the other. And we all get what we want."

"What do you want?"

"Access. You let us use this place for some things." Tony glanced around the storeroom. He lifted a sheet draped over old tin signs and wooden frames. "And we look the other way when you can't pay some bills."

Blaze felt sick. His needs scratched beneath his skin. A thin sheen of sweat broke out along the back of his neck. Blaze wanted to tear Tony apart. But he couldn't help his sickened desperation. Blaze licked his dry lips.

"See, Blaze. We came for good reasons. Huh? Whaddaya think?" Dougie rejoined the discussion. He smiled back at Tony as he moved his sunglasses from his nose to the top of his head.

Blaze broke down. He agreed to the terms of the deal. The gnawing of his addiction hastened the argument in favor of Tony. Blaze would sneak them in and out of the brewery, behind his boss' back. All they wanted was to stow away some "hot" goods and shoot a dirty film occasionally. In exchange for the clandestine space, they would give Blaze the best heroin this side of the world and forgive his debts.

It seemed an easy deal to make.

But what about Matt? After all Matt had done for him, this was how he would repay his kindness?

When Blaze returned from the war, he couldn't find work or a place to live. One look at his stuff bag and shaved head was all it took for doors to slam in his face. Even his folks turned him away when they found the track marks dotting his skin. Just when Blaze had been on the brink of suicide, he had run into Matt in the brewery.

He remembered it like it was yesterday.

Strung out with no options left, Blaze figured he would attempt to drink himself to death. He had been drawn to the brewery, feeling a magnetic pull pulse through his boots. The weathered façade reminded Blaze of a weary sailor's countenance. The cracked shutters like fuzzy eyebrows perched upon sad eyes. An ancient wooden door welcomed him like dry lips accepting a wrinkled cigarette. The massive structure stoic along the dusty landscape of a time that had long ago been forgotten.

And the upstairs window. It stood alone like the third eye chakra of a foreign god, watching over the patrons who defied the signs of lurking darkness within.

Blaze had shaken off the goosebumps crawling along his tanned flesh. He had ignored the sensation of a presence that followed him from behind the warped panes of that solitary window. He had shrugged and decided the brewery was as good a place as any to finish his struggle.

Matt had been covering the bar because Tina, the bartender, had called out sick with "female issues." Matt had engaged Blaze in conversation as he tried to close the brewery that night. Blaze's slurred speech and sad story connected with Matt. His benefactor offered him a place to stay, a simple cot in the back and an honest day's wage if he would promise to work hard and help out around the brewery. Blaze had cried as Matt tucked him in that night.

Once he had saved up some money, Blaze had found an apartment in town where the landlady was too old and blind to realize he had been a soldier. She only cared about the money to support her golden years.

After all Matt had done for Blaze, when nobody else would give him a chance, he would betray the kindness that he had been given. Blaze clenched his fists. Tony's words echoed in the recesses of his mind.

"You didn't survive that war only to come home and be killed, didya?"

Blaze punched a hole in the storeroom wall.

· · · **XXX** · · ·

21

The image reflected in the mirror scared the hell out of him. Blaze wondered how much of the monster that stared back at him was the thing that fed his addiction. Warped angles around his jawline and forehead morphed, adding to the nausea which swirled in his belly. Blaze splashed some cold water on his face, took a deep breath, and did his best to straighten himself before leaving the restroom. Dougie had given him some truly strong "medicine" as a down payment towards their new arrangement.

Blaze opened the restroom door. He glanced around the hallway, careful to avoid Matt. The coast was clear. Blaze returned to the bar to finish his work. When he rounded the corner, Matt waved him over from behind the bar. Blaze blinked hard to clear the fog from his wobbly brain. He smiled at Tina. Matt tossed a filthy dishrag over his left shoulder. He signaled Blaze to follow him into the storeroom.

As they entered, Matt slammed the storeroom door shut. Blaze jumped, but more so in his mind than physically. His body still felt numb and slow from the dose.

"Can I ask you an important question?"

Blaze nodded without removing his gaze from the floor.

"Who were those guys? And why the hell are they back here?" Matt threw the dishrag across the room. The dry rag hardly sailed across the stacks of beer. The ire in Matt's tone scared him. Even though Matt was shorter than Blaze, his stocky build and Irish temper were enough to cause concern.

"Just some friends." Blaze wiped at the sensation of saliva along his lips.

"Just some friends." Matt parroted Blaze. His graying, reddish hair dulled against the hostile flush which filled Matt's angry features. "I have friends, too. I don't show them around the back of the brewery, Blaze." Matt dipped his head, drawing Blaze's attention. "Why were they back here?"

Blaze thought for a moment before responding. He needed to come up with something plausible or everything would implode. No access to the brewery, then no drugs. And he would have to come up with the funds to cover his debt. Quickly.

"Uh, they wanted to understand the business. Um, they might open up a place of their own."

Matt folded his arms across his chest. Experienced muscles twitched along his forearms. His head nodded furiously. "I see. So, you gave them a personal tour so they could figure out how to compete with us and put me out of business. Is that it?" Matt's voice sounded on the brink of outward hostility.

"No, not like that."

"Not like that, huh?" Again, Matt used Blaze's words to taunt him.

"I mean, they were thinking of opening a brewery a couple of counties over. They just wanted to get a simple look. That's all." Blaze dug his hands deep inside the pockets of his threadbare jeans. He felt the tremors working down to his fingers.

Matt walked a tight circle. His breathing came through his nostrils like a bull, heavy and steaming. "I don't know, man. I gave you a chance. You brought people in here without my permission. You shared MY trade secrets. And they didn't look like friends I would want to be seen with in public. I'm not sure what kind of friends these clowns are. You..." Matt stopped mid-sentence and leaned closer to Blaze. "Are you high, man?"

Blaze backed up a few steps. "No, man. I'm clean."

Matt glared. Blaze felt as if his eyes roamed within his soul, searching for the truth. A trail of sweat broke out along his back.

"You better not be getting fucked up on the job. And nobody else gets a fucking tour, you understand me?" Matt poked an iron finger into Blaze's chest.

"Yes."

"Louder. I can't hear you."

"Yes." Blaze elevated his words above the mumbled whisper he originally gave. Matt's authority mirrored the drill instructor's in boot camp. He tried to maintain eye contact with Matt, but, every few seconds, the guilt tugged his attention to sporadic objects around the room.

"I like you, Blaze. I fell for your story and gave you an

opportunity. You became like a brother to me. But I can't have you giving away my business. I've worked too hard to build this place up from nothing, especially to have a junkie Vet blow it for me. I'm fucking pissed, Blaze. Don't mistake my charity for weakness." Matt rubbed his face. "I'll fire you. I'll do it. Don't make me. Don't force my hand. I can deal with slip-ups occasionally. But, if you betray my trust, Blaze, then I will cut you out quicker than you can spit. Am I understood?"

Blaze fought every fiber of his being from collapsing inside his drug-induced blanket. He wanted nothing more than to lie down and sleep off the sweetness flowing in his veins. Blaze needed to control himself, get through the tongue-lashing. Then he could figure out the rest of the plan. In his heart of hearts, Blaze felt sorry for Matt. He knew his addiction would lead him to the betrayal Matt warned him against. Until then, Blaze would lie.

"I'm sorry. Really sorry, Matt. I should've cleared it with you first. I would never give up your secrets." Blaze scratched at the back of his scalp. "I promise. I won't be so stupid again. I'm really, really sorry."

Matt bent to pick up the dishrag. He glowered at Blaze for what seemed an eternity. His finger jabbed Blaze's chest once again, reinforcing his warning.

"I won't hesitate, man. Fuck up, and you're out." Matt slung the rag over his shoulder, nearly running over Tina on his way into the bar.

Blaze attempted to look busy, as if he had been moving supplies around the room the entire time. He didn't want Tina to know he had gotten chewed out. Since he had laid eyes on her, Blaze had had a mild crush on Tina. She was almost a decade older than he was, but she was extremely attractive and had a stunning figure. Blaze had always had something for redheads, even though she was more of an auburn than a true redhead.

"Everything good back here?" Tina looked for a crate of beer mugs.

"Yep. Just doing my job." Blaze's words hung in the air as if he had something else to say but had thought better of it. Tina caught him checking out her rear as she stood up with the crate of mugs.

"Sounded like Matt was upset."

Blaze shrugged off her comment. Tina was either fishing for gossip or she already knew the answer, having overheard Matt's raised voice.

"Oh, we're good now. I just...made a mistake."

Tina slammed the crate of mugs down on a couple of kegs. She neared Blaze. His breath caught in his throat.

"We get that a lot around here. Matt has a habit of getting lots of bugs up his ass." She grinned and snapped her gum. Blaze couldn't help himself. He allowed his eyes to linger on hers for an extended moment. He smiled back.

"I brought my friends back here. Matt didn't like it." Blaze sat back against some pallets. "It was harmless, but I get Matt's point."

Tina slapped Blaze's shoulder. "He'll get over it. A few pints and he'll be humming drinking songs from his ancestors."

They shared a short laugh.

"So how do you know these friends of yours?" Tina tilted her head, adjusting the band which propped up her hair.

Blaze scrambled to come up with a cover story, something that would pass muster should Tina and Matt talk.

"Well," he paused, as if figuring out how to tell her. Suddenly, a detailed lie popped into his head. It was too detailed to be confused for a lie. "I served overseas with Dougie's brother. He didn't make it back. I brought Dougie his belongings." Blaze wrinkled his brow as if he were biting back tears.

Tina ate up the story. "That's so sad. At least *you* made it back, honey." She rubbed his arm with compassion.

Tina left Blaze to finish his work. As she picked up the case of mugs, Tina turned toward Blaze. "Tony is cute, huh?"

Blaze bristled.

"You should've introduced me to him. You know, I used to do some acting back in the day. And Tony offered me a part in a new film he is shooting. How lucky is that?"

Tina hurried from the storeroom, all giddy with potential fame and fortune as a re-discovered movie starlet. Blaze struggled to keep his anger in check. He understood what type of movie Tony was interested in shooting. And Blaze had no intention of letting Tina get caught up in mobster adult filth.

He clutched the end of a pallet so hard, the wood fractured, splinters jamming under his skin. The high he had been enjoying had been overrun with rage.

· · · **XXX** · · ·

Crawling along the stained, gray tiles, Blaze fought the surge of dope flying throughout his system. The needle was still jammed in the crook of his right arm. A trickle of blood leaked from the pinhole surrounding the head of the needle.

Mortars go off all around him. Palm fronds shake like evil banshees trying to scare him from his spot along the jungle floor. Screams behind him reveal one of his comrades is hit. Another shell strikes the earth at his 9 o'clock. The ground rocks beneath him, lifting his body up and slamming him back down. Machine gun fire rips through the greenery ahead. Blaze tucks his head into the soil, a grimy hand holding his helmet to shelter his skull.

RAT-TAT-TAT. RAT-TAT-TAT-TAT-TAT.

Blaze needs to find his platoon. They were separated when the ambush struck. Mulroney and Schwartz were shredded. Mulroney had been pointing out their objective on his soiled map. He was mid-sentence when a heavy round tore his left arm clear of his body. He let loose the most sickening noise Blaze had ever heard before it was cut off by another round straight through his windpipe. Schwartz had been radioing in their coordinates for the potential Pickup Zone when small arms fire peppered his chest. Blaze heard the air hiss from his friend's lungs as he dropped. The recognition of the end evident in Schwartz's expression.

The neon sign in the bathroom window flickered and buzzed. Flashes of blueish-purple refracted off the tile walls.

Blaze wanted to scream. So much terror. But he was afraid the dinks would zero in on his location. He inched along the moist turf, trying to see through the smoke and chaos. Blaze heard his commanding officer barking out orders. Tucking his chin into the dirt, Blaze crawled in the direction of Sergeant Polk. He hoped to re-group with his brothers in arms.

Green vomit spewed, ejecting the remainder of his lunch. Blaze had shared a soup and salad with Tina because he hadn't wanted to take a full lunch hour. He worried Matt would try to rip him a new one for not giving it his all. Blaze had intended to skip lunch and work through until Tina had asked him to keep her company. He figured he would use the opportunity to talk her out of the porn shoot. But he didn't have the courage to bring it up, even though Tina went on and on about her dreams of celluloid stardom.

The Sarge shouted at Blaze. He stood over his prone body, unafraid of the deadly battle surrounding them. He had yelled at Blaze for snaking around on his belly like a coward when they needed to return fire on the ambush. Sergeant Polk ripped a heavy pack off a dead infantryman, inspecting it quickly for damage. Satisfied it was still in working order, the Sarge shoved a flame-thrower into Blaze's hands.

"Burn these fucking gooks out, Match. Don't stop until you smell fried chicken."

Blaze swallowed his fear and strapped on the device. Corporal Streeter lit the end, confirming he was good to go with a definitive nod, and Polk pushed Blaze ahead into a wall of hazy grayness. Smoke irritated his eyes and tree limbs scratched his arms. Blaze triggered the handle, letting loose half a gallon of napalm per second. He trekked forward, the heat singeing his eyebrows with each squeeze of the trigger. Bullets screamed past him as he moved the line of flames forward before fanning the fire outward in a semi-circle of death. He could smell the crisp flesh, the stink of instant decay turning his innards raw. Blaze rounded an edge of dirt mounded taller than the height of an average man. He flamed the top of the hill just as two heads peered over with bayonets at the ready. Their faces melted faster than ice cream on a summer day. Eyeballs rolled away from fried sockets. One man clawed at his face to brace himself against the pain. Instead, his hands came away with a soupy mixture of flesh and blood. The dying shrieks overshadowed explosions and machine guns.

Blaze heard a noise coming from the parking lot. He needed to get to the door before Dougie and Tony got antsy. But his body wouldn't obey his commands. It was too overwhelmed with the bad trip. He croaked out an order for his legs to help him up. The sound, while inaudible in the real world, rammed through his head from one ear to the other like an ice pick.

Something swam in the ether above him. His eyes watered, so he had to blink to clear his vision. What floated along the dirty drop ceiling made no sense to Blaze. It appeared to be a human form, yet it was too fluid to be of real substance.

TINA?

Blaze struggled against gravity. He needed to rise to see what exactly had joined him in the restroom.

TINA?

He swore Tina swam through the air. The face was undoubtedly Tina's, but everything else was…unfinished? His mind reeled to come to terms with his situation. Blaze slammed his eyes shut, trying to force the bad trip to completion. Madness was nearby and he wanted to stave it off until he could finish what he had set out to do tonight.

Be careful, Frederick.

The voice filled his head. Foreign, yet inside his own mind.

NOBODY CALLS ME FREDERICK ANYMORE.

Danger is all around you, Frederick. You must get away while you can.

Blaze fumbled to rub his eyes, instead poking one with an ungraceful finger. The voice had to be another ghost from his tour of duty. But it was unfamiliar.

They're all around you.

WHO?

Blaze drooled. He pulled himself up on his elbows. His neck strained to watch the figure drift all around him. He wished he could reach out and touch it, see if it felt as slippery as it looked. The Tina-shape writhed and undulated as it circled above. Blaze suddenly realized he could see the tiles along the wall through her body. He struggled with his confusion.

The images smacked him across the face, blurring his sense of reality.

A pistol pointed at a scared man. The gun fires, a hole exploding through the scared man's forehead, depositing the milky contents on the wall behind him. A little girl holds a small finger to her lips as if to silence Blaze. Her white dress ruffles in the gentle breeze of a late spring morning. She smiles right before an old sedan speeds into her frail form. A long streak of blood and gore squiggles along the pavement where she had once stood. A woman is brutally carved with a long knife. Her skin is flayed and stripped in long flanks, and then laid atop wax paper stretched along the floor. The woman screams through the gag in her mouth, very much alive while being sliced apart. A dark window with rustic panes of glass. A young man stares out the window as tears roll down his cheeks. He is very depressed; Blaze feels his desperation. Blaze is reminded of the early American Revolution by the attire, a ruffled shirt, stockings and knickers. The young man wipes the tears away with the back of his shirt sleeves. He steps up on a brittle wooden chair, loops a noose around his neck and then kicks away the chair. As he swings and suffocates, the young man watches a young woman in a forest green dress through the window pane. She giggles and holds hands with another young man. She glances up to the window and winks at the hanging man. An oven full of human remains, the meat charred to a blackened crust. An older woman removes the flesh, plating the pieces for a family of strange-looking children. The children dig into their meals with reckless abandon.

Blaze choked on his gorge, the taste of bile thick on the back of his tongue.

WHAT IS THIS YOU SHOW ME?

It is what has been and will always be.

WHERE ARE YOU FROM?

The past and the present and someday, the future.

Blaze hated the riddles. He wished the bad trip would end. The sound of voices in the parking lot outside the bathroom window spurred him on. He climbed to his knees. The apparition ducked into corners, absorbing the darkness, making it more difficult for Blaze to see her.

LEAVE ME ALONE. LEAVE ME ALONE.

The specter dashed into his chest. Blaze felt a fluttering and warmth before an icy chill shot up his spine.

It will be okay. If you walk away.

Blaze gathered enough strength to pull himself up to his feet. His hands rested on his knees to steady his equilibrium. The warning had been clear, but he couldn't understand what any of it meant. His stomach and head met in a death match of wills. Blaze's stomach won out.

Blaze threw up in the sink.

$$\cdots \textbf{XXX} \cdots$$

The storeroom was decked out with drop cloths and chairs. Blaze had been relieved to find that Tina wouldn't be part of tonight's film shoot. He settled into his nerves and asked Tony what the drop cloths were for. Tony said it was important to leave as little mess behind as possible. Again, Blaze felt relieved. He figured the arrangement might end up being quite mutually beneficial. Tony was more considerate than he had originally seemed. Blaze had never considered the potential messes left behind from stag films. All the writhing, sweaty bodies and fluid exchanges hadn't even dawned on him.

Tony had hurried Blaze out of the storeroom as the

actors came in. He said the actors were beginners and got nervous if too many people looked on. Tony thought it would be helpful if Blaze could hang around outside, keep watch on the parking lot in case any groupies or fans found out the shoot was taking place at this secret location. Blaze found it odd since the whole operation was clandestine. However, he understood how loose lips could squash the best laid plans. He took his post in the shadows of the overhead lights, while the cameras and equipment were transported from a rental truck into the building.

· · · **XXX** · · ·

Marcus lingered a moment longer. His fingertip slid along the dried quill ink. The fancy penmanship mirrored the tender message on the parchment.

I'll love you always, my dear.

He choked back his sorrow. He wondered if it had been a ruse all along. Or had she lost interest? Their time apart had been difficult for them both.

The cause was too important. The colonies had found themselves on the brink of turning the corner. Plans had come together, and Marcus had an opportunity of a lifetime. Delivering messages, information vital to the cause, between Philadelphia and New York had increased his visibility among the elite, the true power brokers funding the revolution. Future positions in wealthy organizations had been hinted at, even one offer to apprentice with the esteemed Mr. Franklin at his press. Yet, all the intrigue and danger had kept them apart for nearly a year.

Marcus had longed for her delicate touch, the lilac smell of the fragrance on her kerchief. He had dreamt of his return to her soft kisses for many months. It had never occurred to Marcus that Delilah could have found another. Her letters had sent no such inkling. The words had been as gentle and intimate as if they stood face to face in the dusky shine along the Raritan. The image remained etched upon his memory; their final day together before he had waved goodbye with tears in his eyes.

Now the tears had returned. However, these tears stung where the others had swelled.

Marcus crumpled the parchment in his fist. He pounded his hand on the balsam table.

Future opportunities no longer mattered. Marcus couldn't see beyond his current melancholy. If Delilah wouldn't be at his side, then what use would it be to fight on. Political strife and religious freedoms be damned! The new country's landscape grayed without the rays of sunshine in her precious smile.

The sound of laughter shook Marcus from his depression. The crumpled paper dropped, soundlessly landing on the floorboards. He traced his steps along creaks and knots. As Marcus approached the window, he used tear-dampened fingers to clear aside the burgundy cloth.

Delilah.

His heart pounded with anguish. The beautiful visage had malformed to horror.

Delilah wasn't alone.

Her new love sat next to her. One hand on her lower back. The other caressing Delilah's upturned cheek.

· · · **XXX** · · ·

Something felt wrong. A sudden chill worked its way down Blaze's spine. He shook the ice from his limbs, pacing through the parking lot. A sensation of being watched kept him moving between the cars. His eyes were drawn to the upstairs window above the brewery. A young man stared at him from behind the dirty pane. Blaze shuddered as he recalled the vision of the person who had hung himself. He rushed into the brewery. Blaze wasn't sure if he was going to chase the man out or find a real ghost haunting the place. As he ran across the bar toward the stairs, the sound of crying halted Blaze in his tracks.

The storeroom.

Blaze forgot all about the person upstairs. He followed the hushed tones and whispering. Listening at the storeroom door a moment, Blaze picked up an angry voice, too. He twisted the knob gently, hoping to get a peek without stirring anyone's attention. As the door opened a crack, Blaze felt his tongue dry up.

THIS ISN'T A PORN SHOOT.

To his horror, Blaze stared at the couple. The woman, standing before the seated man, was nude. She cried as she raked a vegetable peeler across the man's stomach. It sliced ragged strips of skins from his trembling flesh. His eyes were wide with terror and pain. A rag was stuffed in his mouth, so his screams remained muffled.

Blaze swallowed hard.

The woman paused, leaning her elbows on her knees as if she caught her breath from carrying heavy sandbags. One of the camera techs ran into view and sliced across the woman's back with a small knife. She reached around at the fresh wound, her head tossed back in anguish.

Tony stood off to the right, arms folded. He smirked as the scene unfolded.

The woman returned to her macabre task.

Blaze swung the door wide.

The hinge squeaked, drawing the attention of all eyes.

The man in the chair fought against his restraints. He pleaded for help with a choked scream. The woman dropped the peeler and ran toward Blaze. Several steps later, she was nearly beheaded by a gleaming machete. She sprawled along the drop cloth, spraying blood. Blaze knew she was dead before she landed, but he rushed forward anyway.

Two of the mobsters grabbed a hold of Blaze while Tony stood before him. Blaze didn't hear Tony threaten him, his eyes drawn to the naked man in the chair. He sobbed. Head sunk down on his chest. Blaze figured the man had given up his fight after watching the actress get slaughtered.

Tony slugged Blaze in the stomach. He bent in half as all the air expelled from his lungs. He wanted to shout at

Tony, but his voice found no power. On his knees, the two mobsters beat Blaze. They stomped him with the heels of their fine, leather shoes. Punches split open his mouth and his eye. Blaze quickly lost his ability to cover himself from the punishment. His body faded into oblivion as the blows kept coming.

The last thing Blaze saw before the world went dark was the man in the chair, eyes pleading for help, right before he was executed.

· · · *XXX* · · ·

The pain was sharp. Blaze awoke to a damp cloth dabbing at his face. It took a moment for his eyes to adjust to the light. Blaze found Dougie hovering over him. He attempted to pull himself up but Dougie held him down with a stern hand. Blaze gave in, deciding his head hurt too much to sit upright.

Dougie chastised Blaze for being stupid. He said Blaze had a good thing now and he would only ruin it if he thought about becoming self-righteous.

"You don't know these people. What do you care what happens to them?"

Blaze wanted to argue but his mouth was pasty with the taste of blood.

"Bad people deserve bad things. You think those folks were innocent?"

He winced away from the damp cloth. Blaze glanced across the storeroom. The place was spotless. The room looked just as it had when his shift had ended. No signs of mobsters or drop cloths or blood.

"Besides, it's not like this is any different than what your country did to you. Am I right?" Dougie sat back on his haunches. "They sent you to the other side of the world to fight for a cause that had nothing to do with us, man. They just threw good kids into the meatgrinder. And for what?"

Blaze groaned. He'd grown sick of everyone's political agendas about Vietnam. Both sides of the argument were right...and wrong. Blaze just wanted to shoot up so he could sink into the inky darkness of his mind. Forget all the pain.

The little girl in the white dress shushed him from the corner.

Blaze blinked. Her image remained. He wondered if he had finally lost his mind. Reconciling all the drug-induced trips and the eerie visions became an exercise in futility.

"They're gonna kill Tina."

Dougie laughed. "Relax, man. Tina's doing a skin flick, not a snuff film."

Blaze pulled himself up on his elbows. "She didn't sign up for this. You lied to her. And to me." He watched the little girl skip rope on the other side of the room. She smiled and laughed, lost in her childhood innocence.

Dougie tossed the damp rag on Blaze's head. He wandered around the storeroom, touching boxes as if he were counting them. "I didn't lie to you, man. I just didn't tell you the whole truth."

"What IS the truth?"

Dougie circled back. "Those people fucked on film. They did a porno." He shrugged and looked at the ceiling, his long hair cascading over his shoulders. "It finished with a snuff film."

Blaze rushed to stand. His head swam, forcing him back to his knees. "Is that how it's gonna end for Tina?" The little girl stifled a laugh. She blew Blaze a kiss.

Dougie smirked. "You got a crush on her, man? You're acting like a schoolboy."

Blaze rubbed his temples. Black dots flashed through his peripheral vision. He groaned a negative response, lying to himself as well as Dougie. "I don't want her to get hurt."

Dougie fired up a cigarette. He offered one to Blaze. Blaze didn't smoke, having given up the habit when he had returned from overseas. Dougie tucked the extra cigarette back into his crushed pack. He tucked the smokes into the back pocket of his faded jeans.

"Tina's not gonna get hurt. Straight sex, man." Dougie bent to help Blaze to his feet. "It's not her first rodeo."

Blaze winced; although, he couldn't discern if the pain was from his body or his heart. He glared at his dealer. Dougie slapped his shoulder.

"Tina's been around, brother. She told us she did some stags to pay for school. I wouldn't force her into anything she wasn't comfortable with."

Blaze grunted. "Yeah, you're a real saint, Dougie."

Dougie held his arms wide. "I'm a survivor, man. Just like you. Anyway, it's not for you to make choices for Tina. Or anyone else."

"What about Tony?"

Dougie exhaled his cigarette smoke. He tapped the ashes on the floor and shook his head. "He's pissed. He wanted to whack you, but I stuck out my neck for you, man." Dougie took a long drag. "I'm running out of excuses for you. The only reason he didn't go through with it is because I reminded him how veterans need time to adjust to regular life again. His Pop went through some…adjustments…when he returned from Normandy. Never underestimate a goombah's affection for his family."

Blaze watched the little girl. She danced and laughed. Then exploded into a splash of blood along the walls and floor. He thought he heard tires screech and thud as a vehicle connected with the weight of something. The little girl. He gritted his teeth, searching for the image to come back to life. As he waited for the little girl to return, a set of fingers crept up from the puddle of blood on the floor. A massacred hand followed the fingers up through the floor. Blaze choked back vomit as his gorge rose.

The woman from his dreams, the one who was being flayed apart, piece by piece, climbed through the puddle. The ends of her severed limbs slapped, like dead fishes, for purchase along the bloody floor. She whispered to Blaze but her request was inaudible. Blaze felt her hopelessness permeate his soul. He started toward her when Dougie interrupted him to say goodbye.

· · · **XXX** · · ·

The next morning, Blaze waited for Tina. He leaned against the brick façade of the brewery, careful to stand within the remaining shadow before noon. He hadn't slept last night, worried about Tina's involvement with Tony. Trying to piece together the horrific images of the brewery added to his restlessness. Something about the people he kept seeing led him to believe he needed to solve their problems. He felt drawn to helping them, yet he hadn't figured out if they were truly ghosts requiring assistance or figments of his imagination. Blaze cursed the heroin in his system for clouding his judgment.

The little girl. The young man. The hacked woman.

WHAT DOES IT MEAN?

Blaze straightened as Tina pulled into the lot. Her sky-blue Mustang showed its age. Unlike Tina. Her cherry hair, stuffed under a white scarf, floated behind her in the breeze. The cats-eye sunglasses hid her hazel eyes. She flashed a smile and waved at Blaze. He waited for her to near before speaking. Tina pursed her lips and lowered her sunglasses to take in his beaten face.

"My-my. Looks like somebody had a rough time with the alley cats."

Blaze squinted against the sun. "Got mugged."

Tina searched his eyes from behind the sunglasses. Her expression told Blaze she didn't believe his story. But he didn't care. He had bigger problems. Keeping Tina away from Tony and the other greaseballs, for instance.

"Matt see your new mug yet?"

Blaze shook his head. "No. Look, Tina. We need to talk."

She began to open the door. Blaze jammed his foot against it to keep her from going inside. Tina shot him a fierce look as if to ask him if he dared hold her up.

"I don't want you hanging out with Tony." He bristled. The words came out easier than he had imagined. Blaze bit his lower lip in anticipation of Tina's response.

"Oh, Blaze. That's sweet of you but I don't need you to check on me. And I'm a big girl. I can decide who I hang around with."

Blaze grabbed her shoulders. Tina dropped her

handbag. Her face flushed with surprise. "I don't want you mixed up with him. Them."

Tina wriggled free of his grasp. She snatched her purse from the pavement, dusting it off. Blaze apologized for his actions. "I'm sorry. I mean, they aren't going to help you get to Hollywood. They're into..." He struggled to finish his sentence. The idea of saving Tina suddenly felt ridiculous. He chided himself for letting his infatuation get the better of him.

"For your information, Blaze, I know what they do. I like that stuff." She licked her painted lips. "I've done much worse to get by."

Blaze felt sick. The thought of Tina having sex on film and enjoying it upset his stomach.

"It's fun and I get to make some extra money on the side. It doesn't hurt anyone."

"It hurts me." Blaze reddened. The truth was out there and couldn't be taken back.

Tina smiled. She rubbed a silky hand down his battered cheek. Blaze winced as her fingers slid across one of his wounds. She pulled her hand back, realizing she had hurt him.

"Oh, sweetie. I had no idea you felt this way." She scanned his face. "I like to have fun. I'm not the settling down type." She pushed Blaze aside so she could go inside. Blaze stared at her ass while she walked to the bar along the back wall. "Besides, I don't shit where I eat." Tina removed her sunglasses and scarf, tucking them into her handbag underneath the bar.

Blaze stomped after her. He realized his boyhood fantasies about her had made him look like a fool. An urge to run away and hide overcame him. Whether she liked him back or not, Blaze had to make Tina understand the danger she was in.

"What if they are more than what they seem?"

Tina chuckled. "You mean because they're Italian." She dampened a rag and got to work wiping down the counter. "I know who they are. I've been around here much longer than you, sweetheart. I've seen them all come and go around here with the billfolds and shiny shoes. Money is money."

Blaze reached across the bar. Tina retracted her arms before he could get a hold of her. To hide his failed attempt, Blaze leaned on his outstretched hands. "They'll kill you. They've done it before. They'll do it again." He wondered why he couldn't make a more convincing argument. Or was she just too pig-headed to listen to him? "Please, listen to me."

They both shifted their attention to the door as Matt arrived. He grumbled under his breath and headed straight to his office with little more than a glance. Blaze kept his face tilted away to avoid Matt's discovery of his injuries.

"Like I said, I'm a big girl, Blaze. I'll be fine. But I appreciate you being like my brother." She winked at him and left him standing with his mouth hung open.

He ran outside for fresh air, afraid he would be sick. The sunshine heated the fluid in his veins. His head swam with thoughts of Tina in compromising positions. Blaze realized he didn't know Tina, or anyone else for that matter, as well as he thought he did.

The sound of shattering glass broke him from his illness. Blaze looked up in time to find the young man plummeting to his death. His body bounced on the pavement. A spreading puddle of blood surrounded the man in the early American clothing. The dead, blackened eyes stared through Blaze's soul. His lips fumbled to gurgle a message, half-drowned by the puddle of his own gore.

We need you.

WHAT DO YOU NEED?

Sacrifice.

WHO'S SACRIFICE?

The killing.

The response confused him. The voice hurt his skull like his brain had swelled to bursting.

DID TONY KILL YOU?

It feeds and it's hungry.

Blaze rubbed his eyes with disbelief.

Help us all.

The whisper lingered upon the wind. Blaze hurried into the brewery before he lost his mind.

· · · **XXX** · · ·

Jackie liked playing outside. She enjoyed the fresh air; the sunlight warmed her skin. Her mother always told her to go outdoors. She didn't like Jackie being in the way whenever the customers came by. Jackie only knew what her mother told her, but she never understood why all the customers were men. They would ring the bell for her mother, all dressed up in suits and strong-smelling soaps. But when they left the house, the customers looked sweaty and tired, carrying their jackets over their arm or slumped over one shoulder. Jackie imagined her mother yelling at the men and striking good deals. It made sense by the sounds coming from the back room.

One of Jackie's favorite activities was skipping rope. She loved to twist the braids beneath her feet as if she were leaping across the Grand Canyon. The sensation of soaring above the earth brought a tickle to her belly. Jackie would skip from one end of the block to the other, sometimes as many as ten times before she would tire. The soreness in her arms and legs never bothered her. The sweating did, though. Her mother said real ladies don't sweat. Jackie worried that she wouldn't grow up to be a lady like her mother if she continued to get filthy in her little dresses. But the fun of jumping around would help Jackie forget her mother's constant warnings.

She sat on the front lawn for a bit to cool off. The grass was littered with little pods which had fallen from the big tree on the edge of the property. Mr. Hendricks next door had taught Jackie how to peel the pods apart with her fingernails. The sticky residue on the inside of the pods would make her scrunch her face. But she loved to stick the pod on the end of her nose and tell the world she was Pinocchio. Jackie always remembered the first time Mr.

Hendrick's had shown her how to do it. He had placed one on his large, reddened nose and then he puffed his cheeks out, rolling his eyes back and forth. It had made Jackie laugh so hard she had peed a little in her underpants (but she hadn't told her mother about that part). Since that day, Jackie pretended to be Pinocchio while she caught her breath.

Jackie spit on her fingers to wash away some of the stickiness. A dog barked from across the street. Jackie stared at the dirty dog, its coat clumped and sodden. It hobbled along, favoring its front right paw as if it had broken its leg. The dog barked again.

Her mother's customer shouted from inside the house. He cursed about the noise the dog had made. Jackie stiffened. The man sounded really angry and she feared he would step outside to give the dog a whipping.

She brushed her dirty hands along her thighs and rose to her feet. Jackie waved the dog to come to her. It ignored Jackie's pleas, sniffing around the parking lot of the brewery across the street. Jackie wondered if the dog was hungry, searching for a dropped morsel on the pavement.

It barked louder.

The man inside cursed again. His voice scared Jackie.

She called to the dog, begging it to come to her. She would find something in the house to feed the doggy.

It sat back on its haunches. The dog licked its lips and barked in a continuous cacophony at nothing in particular.

Jackie wanted to save the dog from getting a beating. She also wanted to feed it and give it a bath with the hose in the backyard. Jackie crept closer to the street. She used her pointer finger to beckon the dog to her side.

It lowered its head and directed its loud barks at her. Jackie heard crashing doors behind her. The customer would come outside and hurt the poor dog, who already looked to be having a bad day.

Jackie hurried into the road. She raised her finger to her lips to shush the doggy before it got itself in trouble.

Jackie never heard the car as it came down the street.

· · · XXX · · ·

The heroin worked its way through his core. It surged faster than he had ever experienced in the past. Dougie had given Blaze some good stuff this time. It fed his synapses, dulling the aches. Blaze stared into the mirror. The creature reflected at him resembled a decaying corpse. He strained to look closer at the image in the glass. The eyes were foreign. Demonic. The monster in the reflection bared its sharp, bloody teeth at him. Blaze projected his anger toward the thing which abandoned the living, usurping his soul.

FLASH

Bombs peppered the hill ahead. The strafing jets, deafeningly loud, obliterated the landscape, charring beast and fauna. The man who had been named after his father, Frederick Matkowski, known to his platoon as "Match" for his hair-trigger temper and for lighting up the jungle with napalm, walked with confidence. The small flames licked at the nozzle of his weapon, hungry for more death. Match, soon to be renamed Blaze by his surviving brothers, searched for gooks among the greenery. He knew they were small and fast like rodents. His eyes watched for quick movements.

He needed to kill.

FLASH

Blaze held on to the sink. His knees weakened as the poison reached his heart, flooding his system through tainted veins. The image in the mirror had morphed back to the man he had come to know. Mixed up and drug-addled. Blaze wanted to cry, sad at the husk of a human which remained behind. His real person had died long ago. In Nam.

FLASH

A head popped up from the earth, ten yards in front of him. A North Vietnamese sympathizer with an AK-47 in his hands. The recognition of his ill-timed ascent clouded the dink's face as he dropped his head back into the make-shift tunnel.

Blaze grinned.

He aimed the nozzle and squeezed the trigger. Flames gushed over the lid of the opening. As fire lit up his irises, Blaze saw burning Charlies climb over each other to avoid the perilous immolation. He kicked up the fiery hatch with his muddy boot, jammed the nozzle below ground level and squeezed off another plume of destruction. The fire sucked the oxygen out of the tunnel, so whatever was not burned would die of suffocation. Blaze enjoyed the sound of terror in the foreign tongue, as the dying cursed the white devil who had brought death to their lands.

FLASH

Blaze noticed the outline of the figure in the shadows behind him.

The woman with the huge knife slicing through her flesh. She screamed silently as an invisible hand worked the blade through jagged slashes in her skin. Blood drained from the open gashes. A stink of death and decay wafted from her wounds. He spun to face her.

The little girl in the dress smiled at him. She raised her finger to her lips to silence him. Blaze grasped at her arms, holding tight before the sedan could run over her again. He screamed into her childishly innocent face. He demanded to know what was happening. Why were they dying over and over? What was wrong with the brewery? Was it cursed? What did they need him to do?

Before he got an answer, the little girl exploded into a fine mist of crimson. It sprinkled Blaze's face. He swiped away at the excess that covered his vision.

WHAT THE FUCK IS HAPPENING HERE?

Something beautiful.

HOW IS THE KILLING BEAUTIFUL?

It is what has been and will always be.

DID YOU FOLLOW ME BACK FROM VIETNAM?

We are everywhere. But mostly here.

WHO THE FUCK ARE YOU?

The past and the present and someday, the future.

NO MORE RIDDLES! SHOW ME WHO YOU ARE!

FLASH

A child cries from the weeds. Blaze turns his attention toward the sound. He moves without reserve as bullets shred the fabric of the vegetation around him. The deafening fray fades into the background, allowing the child to reveal its location. Blaze steps on grass and plants, tamping down a fresh path. He ducks under a limb, the dry leaves tickling his soot-covered face, lapping at his perspiration.

The crying is close.

Blaze steps through, into a game trail where an overturned basket rests in the dust. The baby's dying grandmother blinks up at him. Her eyes glazed over. A drizzle of red along the corner of her lips. Her hand reaches toward the crying child.

He watches. The fragility of life rushes to his mind. All the killing. Dying. What was it for? He couldn't answer the question even though it gnawed at him every day in the jungle.

He watches. The baby's face is beet red, tempered by the need to be held. Cared for. Its cries becoming more desperate with each passing second.

He watches. The grandmother whispers in her native tongue. Blaze can't understand a damn word she says. But he gets the meaning, nonetheless.

Please don't kill my grandchild.

Blaze takes an eternity to cement his next move. Should he kill the baby first so the dink's last memory on this earth is of her burning grandchild? Or should he put the old hag out of her misery, ending her pain, and sparing her the evil he will do to the innocent child? Either way, the baby had to die. If it lived, it would grow up to be one of them. Fate had been determined when the grandmother took a round in the gut.

He smiled. Pointed the nozzle. He watched.

He pulled the trigger.

FLASH

WHAT DOES THIS MEAN?

It will be okay. If you walk away.

Blaze puked across the floor. He dropped to his knees,

the cords on his neck straining at his retching.

I'M NOT WALKING AWAY.

He wanted to walk away but something deep within urged him to figure this out. An electrical current bolted through his limbs. Blaze reeled at the fire inside his chest. Every fiber tingled as the energy drank of his being.

If you refuse to walk away, then you will die like the others.

Blaze gasped. Saliva hung from his open mouth.

I HAVE TO SAVE THEM FROM THIS EVIL.

Laughter filled his ears.

You have evil in your heart, Frederick.

YOU DON'T KNOW ME.

The horrors of Vietnam resumed like a film reel in his mind. Each soul he had reaped returned to show him what he had done, but from their point of view. He wanted to turn away from what he saw. The pain of the truth too real for him to accept.

He smiled. He laughed. He enjoyed.

The killing.

I HAD A JOB TO DO!

Yes, and you excelled at it.

Blaze rested his forehead against the cool tile floor. He cried. He asked the spirits in the ether how he could have become such a monster. Everything had changed when Blaze had landed on that foreign soil. It had been a dreamscape.

A nightmare.

I WILL FIX WHAT I HAVE DONE. YOU'LL SEE.

You are part of the problem. Your blackened heart has awakened the dead.

FLASH

Blaze kicked open the door. Tina shrieked, surprised at his sudden entrance. She is bent over a stack of crates. The sweaty man behind her pulls out, holding his hands in the air as if caught red-handed. A lanky guy with a beatnik beard looked up from his camera. He shouted something at Blaze. Tina pointed at him, commanding him to leave immediately.

The rage flowed like water from an open spigot. Blaze stepped forward. The sweaty guy began to look for his trousers. He appeared to have no interest in sticking around to find out how upset the psycho "boyfriend" would be. The lanky cameraman pointed a bony finger at Blaze, complaining that he had interrupted a great scene.

Blaze picked up a full keg and used it to smash at the face of the cameraman, who absorbed the blow with a thudding crash to the floor. The keg felt too light in his hands to be full, but Blaze's anger aroused a superhuman strength. He brought the keg down with all his might, erupting the cameraman's head like a rotted pumpkin from a Halloween night porch.

Tina screamed, covering her breasts with one arm.

Sweaty guy decided against finding his slacks. He sprinted for the storeroom door. Blaze intercepted the man. He clutched the man's throat, digging his fingernails into his skin. Sweaty guy fought against the tight grip without success. Blaze slammed the man's slick body into the wall. His eyes rolled in their sockets as his head took the brunt of the attack. Sweaty guy used his scissoring feet to kick at Blaze. A flailing foot landed a hard shot in Blaze's shin. The sharp pain caused Blaze to loosen his grip. As sweaty guy slipped down, he hurried around Blaze, running for the door to escape. Blaze quickly pursued him, tackling sweaty guy from behind as he reached the door. The two of them crashed to the floor, grappling for the upper hand. Blaze quickly maneuvered into position so that he could wrap his arm around sweaty guy's neck. The choke hold applied, sweaty guy grunted and gasped as he struggled for air. He put up an enormous fight, swinging his head backwards into Blaze's face, using his elbows to connect blows into Blaze's ribs. However, it was to no avail. Slowly, sweaty guy's resistance faded as he neared unconsciousness. Blaze added a final touch by wrenching sweaty guy's neck hard. A loud cracking noise echoed across the storeroom signaling sweaty guy's broken neck.

Blaze gasped for oxygen. He realized that Tina had

continued to scream at him throughout the entire struggle. His eyes rounded on her, finding Tina holding herself, crying and shaking. He went to Tina, authority and purpose in his steps.

"I told you not to do this." Spittle flew from his lips.

"What have you done?" Tina's words came out in hyperventilated bursts.

"You didn't listen to me."

"You...you..." She pointed a shaky finger at the bodies behind him.

"I thought you were better than this." He felt tears brim his eyelids.

Tina backed away. Her expression morphed from horror into fear.

"Don't hurt me. Please. Don't hurt me."

Blaze stepped closer. "You were so sweet. So nice to me."

Tina shook her head, one hand held out to keep him at bay while her other arm covered her breasts. Blaze grabbed her by the shoulders and tossed her across the floor. She landed hard.

His mind replayed the scene with the young man in the upstairs room. Watching his lover through the window. With someone else.

"You cheated on me."

Tina climbed to her feet. She glanced around at her options for escape.

"Blaze, no."

"You betrayed me."

"No."

Blaze closed the gap. He backhanded Tina's face. She faltered against a stack of pallets. Her hand flew to her reddened cheek, a small trickle of blood along her lower lip.

The young man stood behind Tina, a raw scar rounded his neck where the rope had been. Blaze nodded at him. The young man nodded back.

Blaze rubbed his own neck. It burned as if he, too, had recently been hanged. He reached out for Tina. She shoved her hands against his chest, attempting to stay out of his reach.

The young woman looked over her shoulder. Blaze's eye connected with hers as he looked down on her from the ancient pane of glass upstairs.

She smirked at him.

Blaze dug his thumbs into Tina's eyeballs. She shrieked louder than the firefights he had been involved in during the war. He pressed harder, blood and gelatinous fluids oozed from the tortured sockets. Splatter coated his vision. Tina clawed at Blaze's face, her fingernails carved fresh grooves of blood. Blaze forced his thumbs deeper until they poked through the thin, muscular membrane behind her eyes. Having reached her brain, his fingers ended Tina's life. Her body crumpled to the floor.

Blaze stared at his hands, inspecting the gore that remained beneath his fingernails.

The young man smiled at Blaze.

He felt a presence to his right. Blaze turned his attention to find the little girl standing by the door.

She raised her finger to shush him.

· · · XXX · · ·

"What the fuck, man!"

Dougie screamed across the storeroom. Blaze jumped at the sharp tone in his dealer's voice. He fought the urge to yell back at Dougie. Instead, he opted to quietly drift back into his trip. The carnage surrounding him pleased his broken spirit. It had been cathartic.

"You've lost your fucking mind!"

Blaze suddenly felt awake. He looked around the room.

This hadn't been a trip.

He had really slaughtered them.

Tina.

Dougie charged at Blaze. He shoved Blaze hard, knocking him backwards. Blaze had been surprised at the strength his scrawny, hippie friend had. He never would have surmised that a bag of skin and bones could summon such force. Dougie's sunglasses skittered off his face.

"You did it now, Blaze. I can't help you clean up this shit." Dougie bent to retrieve his sunglasses. He placed them on the top of his head. Blaze wondered why hippies wore sunglasses at night. It didn't make any sense.

Three mobsters funneled into the storeroom behind Dougie. One of them was as large as a bull. His neck was wider than a truck bumper, his turtleneck sweater straining to keep its shape. The other two men wore tight-fitting leather jackets that creaked each time they moved.

Blaze blinked. He felt as if several gallons of ice water had been dumped on his head. The delicious, ethereal cocoon of his high dissipated into the rafters. His wounds suddenly reminded him of the reality he had awakened to. The itch of needing more heroin rummaged under his skin like thousands of ants.

"We're both dead, man. We're fucking dead!"

Blaze stared beyond Dougie at the young man. He understood the young man was dead. Had been for many years. The early American garb. The ancient glass window pane. Yet, somehow, the ghost of the young man had reached across two centuries to influence Blaze to exact revenge. Blaze closed his eyes and shook his head to clear the cobwebs. He argued with himself that it had simply been the drugs, and his damaged psyche from the war, that had caused the destruction. Not a ghost.

The little girl smiled at him from the doorway.

Blaze shook his head. "No. No."

Dougie pulled a revolver from the waistband in his faded jeans. He pointed it into Blaze's face. The muzzle still warm from his trousers.

"Tony's gonna kill us both, man. No way is he gonna let this slide. You fucked me, man. You fucked me!" Dougie pressed the gun harder into Blaze's cheek.

Blaze stared at Dougie. He tried to comprehend how he had gotten here. Images of him riding his first bike as a youngster and going to his first school dance replayed in his mind. Flashes of killing from Vietnam smacked him in between cherished memories of life before he went overseas. It had all been so simple back then. He had a family. Friends.

His parents refused to open the screen door. They stood inside, condemning him for sinning by taking another human's life. He had pleaded with them that he had had a job to do. They didn't understand why he hadn't run away to Canada like the neighbor's kid. They blasted him when they found the pockmarks along his veins, scabbed up and raw. Another sign of sin.

It had been more than a job though.

He had liked it.

The killing.

The smell of fear.

The hopelessness in the eyes of his enemy.

The aftermath and horror.

Blaze teared up. His vision blurred.

It will be okay. Close your eyes and come with us.

Dougie ranted on about how much money Tony had invested in his exploitation films. How much Tony stood to make off this deal, even with supplying Blaze and Dougie with free dope.

You should have listened. We warned you to walk away.

I DIDN'T UNDERSTAND YOU THEN.

Do you understand now?

YES.

Well, it's too late. You brought your evil to their hands.

I'M NOT EVIL.

The laughter.

I'M NOT EVIL.

You fool yourself. You believe in an ideal, but you have proven the opposite.

I DID WHAT I HAD TO SO I COULD SURVIVE.

At first. Then you crossed the line into madness.

NO.

They knew what you could do. It's what brought you here.

NO.

They showed you their pain. And you sympathized with them.

NO.

You connected with them.

I THOUGHT THEY WERE BAD TRIPS. I THOUGHT IT WAS THE HEROIN.

The high only thinned the veil. It brought you closer to them.

Blaze dropped to his knees. Above him, Dougie yelled some more before stuffing his pistol back into his waistband. Blaze only half listened to Dougie apologizing for having to kill him. He explained it was his only option to keep Tony from whacking him. He said it was only business, but Blaze had made it more than just business with this mistake.

Blaze rested his face in his hands. He apologized to a God he used to believe in but had long ago forgotten after all he had seen. All he had done. He tried to will his regrets across the universe to his parents so they could live their final days in peace. It wasn't their fault. He cried harder for what he had done to Tina. She had been so beautiful. And kind. Always there to listen to Blaze and encourage him on bad days. Looking out for him, knowing what hell he had been through. He had repaid her kindness with violence. Hatred. Jealousy.

Dougie ordered the men who had followed him inside to take Blaze out. He said to make it extremely painful, as retribution for ruining everything. Blaze lifted his head so he could look his killers in the eyes. He needed them to see what he had seen when he had stolen lives.

A steel blade gleamed in the fluorescents before plunging into his stomach. The knife hurt more as it slid out of his skin than it had going in. Blaze felt the flesh clasp at the blade, not allowing it to pull away freely. He stared at the face of the mobster in the leather jacket. The man's face had been replaced by the woman who was sliced apart. She grinned at him. She whispered thanks for helping her. Blaze felt particles of his soul drift from his wounds. The remnants flew into her mouth, giving her more sustenance.

The little girl stood by the door. She smiled at Blaze and winked.

The knife penetrated his body dozens of times. In between stabs, the other leather coat mobster pulled a cord tight around Blaze's throat. His hands flew up automatically to fend off the choking. He felt the burn of the cord as it dug into his flesh. Blaze's eyes were tightly closed, but he still saw the young man off to the side. The specter fed on the remains of Tina's corpse. He turned a blood-soaked grin toward Blaze. A slight nod and then the young man again turned his attention to the rotten meal beneath him.

You've made them stronger.

Blaze gasped for air. The desperation to breathe overrode any pain associated with the stab wounds which continued to sap him of blood and life.

Now they will accept you as one of their own.

He wished for one final trip to numb his pain. To take him away to someplace far from reality. Life was too painful. Too hard.

The little girl was by his side. She squatted low and tilted her head as if she were trying to figure out what Blaze was thinking. It appeared to be an inquisitive look. With a touch of madness.

The cord released from his throat. The knife ceased its slashing. He choked on the newfound oxygen which rushed through his nostrils. Blaze spit up blood. He rolled his tongue along the back of his teeth, tasting the metallic flavor. The pain of his injuries was so intense that it replicated the high of his addiction. It overwhelmed his senses with a calm acceptance of his fate. His sins needed to be cleansed. The man with the stretched-out turtleneck sweater stepped forward. Dougie pointed down at Blaze and spoke to the hefty hitman. Blaze didn't hear what Dougie said. The only sound pumping through his ears was the voice that had visited him time and again.

It will be okay.

I DON'T WANT TO DIE.

Death is a passing only. From one life to another.

DEATH IS FOREVER.

They scare you into believing that. But, in death, you will live again.

I'M NOT READY TO DIE.

Are you ready to be born again?

Blaze felt his body jerk about. He shifted his focus to the man in the sweater who now rummaged through his stomach as if he were looking for the prize in the bottom of a Cracker Jack's box. The man removed yards and yards of intestines. He'd tug them up and out, holding them aloft like a proud butcher over his sausage. Casting his intestines to the floor with a splat, the man yanked on one of his kidneys, twisting it until it tore free with a bloody rip. He shook the gore from his hands like he had just picked up after his dog without a paper towel.

Blaze closed his eyes again. He folded inside his mind, revisiting battles and failures. He'd finally reached a point where he hoped his life would disappear as quickly as possible. He understood this was a fight he wouldn't walk away from. A war where he had become the casualty instead of the survivor. Blaze knew the underlying current throughout this world. His parents and church had taught him it was love. Love made the world go 'round. Love one another. But the truth had been revealed. Love was a drug to seduce mankind just like heroin.

Evil is what the world was made of. Evil made man turn against his neighbor. Evil tricked everyone into believing they were different. Better. But the truth was much more real. The darkness crept in to shadow the light. Evil used the shadows to hide and slowly tear away the fabric of life.

Evil had been all around.

Forever.

A lone tear ran down the side of his face.

Blaze released his final breath as he stared at the little girl, still squatting next to him.

Still hushing him.

· · · **XXX** · · ·

Tony had been furious with what he had found at the brewery. He had scheduled time to drop by and check on his investment. The snuff film they had finished at the new location had already proven lucrative, netting a few thousand dollars in his own pocket, after paying his vig to the head of The Family. Plus, he had taken care of Carmine and Lucille DeFrancesco with the same stroke. Using them as the "actors" had eliminated any possibility of them cooperating with the Feds about his involvement in the Capuano murders. When Tony and his crew arrived at the brewery, they had strolled in on a high note. Until they had found the mess.

Dougie had apologized profusely. He claimed the veteran had gone mental and wiped out the broad and his film crew. He explained how it would never happen again and he had done his part to take out the nutjob soldier. Tony gritted his teeth as he listened to the kid beg for forgiveness. While Dougie rambled on, Tony had decided how to handle the cleanup. It would be nothing personal, but Dougie had to go. If Tony were honest with himself, he had only kept the hippie on because he kissed Tony's ass so well. From a business standpoint, Dougie's profits were slowly drying up as his clientele overdosed or went to jail. Tony's other distributors were much more profitable, electing to wholesale smack to dealers who then handled the problems with their own distribution channels. Much cleaner for Tony and it provided more of a cushion between his ass and the street. Dougie's last few *ideas* had ended in financial losses. But Tony loved his latest idea. The underground films tapped an insatiable market Tony hadn't realized was desperate for fresh creations.

Tony rested his hand on Dougie's shoulder. He spoke softly and explained to him that it wasn't personal. Business was business. And Tony had to cut his losses. He couldn't afford to have any loose ends. He kissed Dougie's cheek, pulled his jacket lapels tight and made his way to the door. There were plenty of locations they could tap for their monetary gains. There was no lack of desperate folks who would do anything to save their asses from overdue debts or to get their hands-on whatever vice they had to have in order to satisfy their problems. The brewery was caput. Once the mess had been cleaned up, Tony wouldn't dare return to the scene, giving the fates a chance to catch up to him.

He nodded at Salvatore as he crossed the threshold to the parking lot. The door closed behind. The mumbled tones of pleading and begging relaxed Tony. Gunshots reverberated inside the building. His men emptied their guns on Dougie and his three men.

Tony reached into his coat pocket. He pulled out the gold tin that held a row of his favorite smokes. He enjoyed the taste of Lucky Strikes. His old man had sworn by them when he returned from World War II. Tony liked to think he carried on his father's traditions by smoking his favorite brand, God rest his soul. He lit the tip and shook out the match. The sulfuric taste burned through the cherry on the end. Tony released a long plume of smoke through his nostrils while he picked a loose leaf of tobacco from his lips. He waited patiently as his boys finished the killing and then picked the bodies clean of cash and identification. Tony was both careful and resourceful.

A chill tickled his spine. He found it strange since the night wasn't cool enough to deliver such a reaction. He couldn't help but feel as if he were being watched. Tony glanced around the parking lot and up the street. Nothing stood out. The feeling lingered and pricked at the back of his neck. Tony ground out his cigarette under his expensive loafers. He stared up at the old window on the second floor.

The window was dark.

Something about the frame of glass gave Tony the creeps. He couldn't shake the sensation that there had been a pair of eyes up there. He shook away his paranoia, blaming his mother's old-world superstitions and tales. She had used stories of witchcraft and vampires to scare Tony into doing his chores or going to bed early. He missed his mother dearly, but he didn't miss her guilt trips. Tony certainly missed her cooking, God rest her soul.

Tony made a sign of the cross and kissed the gold ring on his pinky, the one with Jesus on the cross. He opted to wait in the car instead of standing in view of the creepy upstairs window. Tony sat in the back seat of the Cadillac, lighting another cigarette.

He peeked up at the window one more time, sure he would find the devil staring back at him.

· · · **XXX** · · ·

The smell of gunpowder hung over the bodies like a smoky mist. It overpowered the ancient musk of beer and dust. Nothing stirred within the bowels of the brewery. Not even the rodents.

A door upstairs slowly creaked its way open. The hollow echo of boots making their way down the wooden steps drowned out the sound of blood dripping from fresh wounds. The footsteps approached the center of the storeroom.

You should have listened. We warned you to walk away.

The unearthly voice waited through the silence.

In death, you will live again.

Again, silence.

The disembodied speaker drifted toward Blaze's corpse. It hovered above, drawing the remnants of life particles that had not yet dissipated into the ether. The essence fed its core, brightening the source of all that had laid in wait, hiding for an eternity to be rewarded for its patience. Its obedience.

There would be more work to do. The demons understood these players would be replaced. A never-ending trail of souls would cross the threshold, bringing new horrors.

As it had always been. And like it would always be.

It moved throughout the room, pecking at the remains like a buzzard on a hare in the desert. The feeding would only satiate the hunger temporarily. The demons willed more souls to enter, beginning the arduous task of drawing fresh prey to its talons. It hoped the next meal would come sooner rather than later. The feedings needed to increase in size and frequency if the beast was to continue its development.

· · · XXX · · ·

Autumn had begun to take hold, caressing the town with a brisk wind. Mahogany and amber leaves crinkled along the sidewalks in a mindless search for a place to rest. The town grew quiet as daylight hours gave way to darkness. While the seasons churned around it, one thing remained constant, defying the progression of life.

The brewery.

The brick façade braved the silence that had fallen on the old building. Legends of murders had bolstered the brewery's reputation as a den of evil. The owner struggled to keep the doors open once the public fervor and looky-loos died down. The lore had been dark enough to frighten away not only customers but also prospective buyers. Eventually, Matt had to walk away, a balance sheet in ruin and a bank account smaller than the critters that roamed the walls, free of distraction.

Travelers drove past with hardly a glance at the haunted building. Children chose to walk on the opposite side of the street lest they fall prey to the spirits left behind. Rumors of apparitions in windows and shadows along walls provided incentive for avoidance, and fodder for local authors. Teens brave enough to face dares from their peers had scrawled satanic symbols and macabre words to reinforce the building's reputation. One wisecracker had attached a bright yellow crime scene tape across the main entrance. A frayed and loose end waved at passersby.

THE LAST TAPROOM ON THE EDGE OF THE WORLD

(II)

*D*EMONS.

"I'm sorry, Mr. McDaniel," Nolan said, dropping his pen on the pad and looking up from his notes. "I don't think the ramblings of a heroin-addicted Vietnam *hero* are really going to convince my readership of what took place there."

Paul grinned, then put the glass to his lips. He sipped slowly as he studied the young writer.

Nolan sighed. He'd come here for something more than tall tales and cheap ghost stories. Irrefutable proof that the remains of Bayberry Bluff were haunted. That the bones of that place were still alive. What McDaniel had given him so far was a story about demons and visions of Hell from someone who had clearly been going through a rough time, battling his *inner* demons.

Perfect if this were a Hollywood movie, Nolan thought, *and not a book on true-life hauntings.* He checked his watch. An hour had passed. No one else had entered Paul's bar, not a single customer. Outside, the storm continued to rage on, the rainfall showing no signs of slowing down. Behind the bar, Sylvester washed the same ten glasses over and over, pretending to keep himself busy. The small television in the corner played a local college basketball game, but the signal kept getting scrambled, freezing every ten minutes or so.

"Are you saying that you're not buying into the legend, Mr. Nolan?"

Nolan hated the way the man was smiling. His lips were crooked, all wrong. Like they weren't attached to his face. He also acted like he knew the story was bullshit, subterfuge, a method of toying with him. Putting him on. Trying to make a fool out of him by feeding him a bunch of bogus stories, stuff his publisher would balk at. He supposed the story of Blaze was partially true—maybe there was a man who had gone by that name, who'd worked in the place that had once housed the criminally insane. The mob aspect also could have checked out. During his limited research, Nolan had discovered the Italian mafia had sunk its roots in the area surrounding Bayberry Bluff. Drugs and prostitution rings. It was conceivable they were shooting underground pornography too.

Maybe it's not all bullshit. Like that old adage—every fable comes from a shred of truth.

"No, not at all," Nolan said, taking a sip of beer. It had a sweet, fruity flavor, though the beverage was full and hazy. Paul had called it a New England IPA, though—not being a big-time beer drinker—Nolan hadn't the slightest idea what that meant. Beer was usually beer, but this— this tasted excellent. "I think most of it will check out, but—"

"Check out?"

Nolan frowned. "Yes, well, these stories are good and all, but they need to be credible. Reliable. Can't be pure fiction."

"So, you're calling me a liar?"

"No," Nolan chuckled. "Not at all. Just, in journalism, we need to verify the facts, nail down the details. Everything needs to check out. Be corroborated. I suppose you don't have references I can check with, do you? People who were there in the seventies? Someone who worked with Blaze? Knew him?"

Paul leaned across the table. "Let me tell you something, Mr. Nolan. Not everything in this world can be truly explained. Verified, like you said. Sometimes, you just gotta believe."

Again, Nolan tittered behind a breath. "Yes, that's all

well and good, but what I'm writing can be classified as non-fiction. Meaning, it actually happened."

Paul eyed him. Nolan wasn't sure if the man would explode with laughter or flip the table. He knew he'd insulted him, and he couldn't blame the guy for having hurt feelings. But still—facts were facts, and stories were stories, and, if he wanted to hit the best-sellers list, he needed to be as factual as possible. Stretching the truth a little wouldn't hurt, but telling stories that had never happened, flat-out *tall tales,* well, that would bury him behind the towering, competitive wall of literary fiction in Barnes and Noble. He'd be lucky to sell a hundred books that way, worldwide. No, his publisher wanted real-life accounts. *Expected* it. That stuff sold like the newest iPhone. Hell, his first two books were already on their fifth printing.

Paul twiddled his thumbs. "Didn't you write a book on the Denver Demons? About that little boy in Colorado who claimed he was possessed by a hundred spirits?"

"Yeah. So?"

"And you're gonna sit there and tell me that was a hundred-percent *factual?*"

Nolan nodded, squinted in *well-you-got-me-there* fashion. "I see your point, but we had witnesses other than the boy himself, and his friends provided reasonable accounts. Family members. Third-party witnesses, doctors and schoolteachers, none of whom stood any chance of financial gain, provided testimonies. Swore they saw the boy levitate above his bed. Heard him speak dead languages. You know, stuff like that."

"Hm." Paul considered this. "Well, I don't believe I have any such witnesses. Except, maybe old Dusty."

"Old Dusty?" He wasn't sure where he was going with this, but it sounded like he was shoveling more manure. Nolan could almost smell the fodder. *How much more do I listen to before I say* thanks, but no thanks?

Just then, thunder crashed and the lights flickered, buzzing with the threat of darkness. Things were still scary outside, but it seemed like the worst was yet to come. He figured he'd wait out the storm. Listen to a few made-up stories, even if he couldn't use them. Maybe, just maybe, Paul McDaniel could tip him off to some useful information, stuff he *could* include in the new book.

The new book.

His dream project.

Every time he thought about holding that new manuscript, he instantly saw his name on the New York Times Best-sellers list. The vision was so real he could almost smell the fresh ink.

"Did you hear me?" Paul asked.

Nolan shook his head. "I'm sorry, what?" Paul had been speaking, but Nolan hadn't heard a word. His delusions of grandeur had stolen him away from the bar.

"We can go visit him if you like." Paul swigged the last mouthful in his glass, dropped the empty on the table. "It'll be good to see my old friend again."

"Um? Now?" He glanced outside again. The storm was in full force. Wind and water dominated the outdoors. He supposed they could drive in it, but it was probably safer if they stayed in. Especially since they had a few beers in them.

"Sure. Now is as good a time as any."

"But... the storm?"

Paul waved off his concern. "It'll pass. Storms always do."

Nolan shrugged. "Well, all right. I'm game if you are." He wasn't sure, but the beers were probably responsible for his being so agreeable.

The old man laughed at that, which, for some reason, made Nolan uncomfortable. A part of him couldn't wait to get out of Ocean View. Hit the road. Do some real research for his future moneymaker. The other part—the smarter half—knew staying inside was the safer, better option.

"I gotta hit the head before we bounce," Nolan said, pushing himself up from the table. His legs felt a bit wobblier than he had anticipated. *Goddamn lightweight.*

After two beers, he should have been fine. Good enough to drive. Good enough to walk a straight fucking line. But, then again, this wasn't some light beer, something that tasted like carbonated water. It was a little more potent. More delicious too.

He made for the bathroom in the corner of the bar, Paul's snickers following him the entire way. He still didn't trust the guy. He half figured he was putting him on, but he'd come all the way from New York, already had his hotel booked in town, so what else was there to do? He had committed this much time and energy already, why not hear what the guy had to tell him?

He closed the bathroom door behind him, locked it, unzipped his jeans, and pissed freely into the cloudy water of the toilet. A yellow circle stained the toilet's porcelain throat, and he figured cleanliness was the least of Paul McDaniel's concerns, which suddenly made him second guess those beers. If this was the condition of what was visible to the customers, Nolan didn't want to think about the status of the rest of the place, specifically, the area where the beer was brewed. He wasn't an expert, but Nolan knew sanitation was a huge part of the process. Any bacteria that got into a batch of brew could get someone seriously sick.

He debated whether to throw up the beer Paul had given him.

After he was finished, he made sure to thoroughly wash his hands, slathering his hands with soap, thankful the old brewmaster had at least provided some.

Just then, the lights flickered in unison with another thunderous crash from the clouds. When they came back on, a woman was standing behind him. Her hair was matted with blood. Red streaks dissected her face, crisscross patterns of crusty crimson. Her eyes were missing. Bruises peppered her face, shaped like rows of knuckles. She was wearing a shirt that had Lost Demon Brewing written across it. Blood flecked her entire body, every visible inch. She mouthed something, her lips working like a puppet without a master. No words were spoken aloud, and Nolan had always been terrible at reading lips.

He was too frightened to try anyway.

The lights flickered again, and she was gone.

He jumped, his back smacking against the wall. He folded to the floor, fear causing his entire body to shake. Even though he'd just emptied it, his bladder filled again.

A knock on the door.

Nolan's heart skipped, rattled around in his chest.

"You all right in there, writer dude?" he heard Paul ask.

Nolan was too scared to reply. He opened his mouth, but there were no words. No words for what he'd just seen. What he'd just witnessed.

Since writing about the supernatural, he'd never experienced anything that could be considered as such. Until now.

He didn't want to rise from the floor. He felt comfortable down there. Safe.

"Hey, Nolan? You fall in or what?"

"J-just a minute!" He closed his eyes, gathered himself. His thoughts swam.

It couldn't have been real. It was my imagination. The story, it got to me. It wasn't real, but it got to me.

He used the wall to pull himself up. Walking over to the mirror, he made sure the woman's reflection was gone.

It was.

He washed his face with cold water, dried it with the available paper towels. Once he felt good enough to walk, he opened the door and stepped back into the bar.

Paul was waiting for him, his rain slicker already on, the hood pulled up over his head.

"Jesus," the old man said. "You look like you've seen a ghost, huh?"

Nolan didn't find that very comical. Paul flashed him a knowing smile, and Nolan wanted to accuse him of something—what exactly, he didn't know. *Harboring ghosts?* That sounded ridiculous. *Spiking the beer with some sort of hallucinogen?* That was more likely, but he had no proof. And, like the good journalist he was, he wasn't about to accuse anybody of anything without the evidence to back it up. That would be irresponsible.

He'd do his work, though. He'd go with Paul to see Dusty, whoever he was. He'd listen to his story, gather all the information.

He'd write his fucking book on Bayberry Bluff, the legend of that place.

He'd make his million. TV deals. Movie stars. That walk up the red carpet. He could see it now, as clear as he'd seen the dead girl in the mirror.

"Yeah, you don't look so good, all right," Paul told him. "Guess I'm driving."

Nolan agreed and took a step toward the coat rack.

"On the way I'll tell you all about Dusty and what that son of a bitch did. It was the 80s... and boy, you should have seen the place..."

HAVE A DRINK ON ME

I TAKE THE corner stool. It's early yet and I have my pick of seats around the bar, but I always pick the corner stool if it's open. It's the perfect position in any bar and I mean *any* bar.

Doesn't matter if it's an L-shaped bar and you had the outside corner or a straight bar and you're tucked in to the last stool between the bar and the wall, the corner stool always offered the best vantage point. If the place is hopping, the corner always has all the action. If the place is seedy, the corner always offers the best vantage point to spot trouble early.

This is my first time in the bar. I'm not sure if it's a dive or alive but I've got the corner stool, so it doesn't matter which way the night goes. There is plenty of night left seeing as it's not even prime time yet.

I've had a bad time of things for a while now, long enough not to remember exactly how long things haven't been good. I'd been driving east for quite some time, headed for the shore, before I realized I needed a drink. This place grabbed my attention. The 'BAR' sign out front looked out of place on a building that otherwise looked like it could have been a busy factory in the industrial age or one of those crazy mental facilities you always see them frequent on those stupid ghost shows.

I like a bar with character, and this had character in spades. And it was a good thing too because it didn't offer much else. Inside it's a big open space. A concrete room with a bar built into it as an afterthought. It echoes inside and reminds me of the sound of the dead calling from beyond. There isn't enough action to fill the big space. I kind of hope things will change for the better soon because, despite its shortcomings, there was something about the atmosphere that I found attractive.

"Lemme get a Bud. Draft." I call to the bartender who only looks my way to acknowledge my patronage.

The bartender wrinkles his nose, "No Bud here." He nods to a chalkboard hung up over the bar.

I glance up and see a tap list on a slab of black slate. Indeed, there was no Bud to be found. There was no Miller, Michelob, not even a Pabst. Instead there are names like Salty Serpent Pale Ale and Sand Dooms IPA and Men In Black N' Tan.

I'm not sure what the hell is going on at this bar, but I know I'm thirsty. I tell the bartender: "I dunno, just gimme a beer. Whatever ya got that's beer."

The bartender's shoulders lift with a silent chuckle and a nod. He grabs a glass, places it under one of the taps, tilting it at a 45-degree angle. As the liquid gold dispenses from the tap, the bartender maneuvers the glass straight up and down until the creamy head crests the top. He places the glass in front of me, a rivulet from the foamy head slithers down the frosted glass. The perfect pour.

I ask the bartender if I can run a tab, placing a few dollars on the bar top as a tip for pouring the first beer of the day so perfectly. The bar may be a bit run down looking but what it lacks in decor it makes up for in professionalism.

"Haven't seen you around here before." The bartender says, "Can I trust ya with a tab?"

It's an odd question; it says he doesn't trust me but is leaving the question of my creditworthiness in my corner.

I add a twenty to the tip. "Yeah, I'm good for it."

The bartender nods. He scoops up his tip and down payment on the tab and sticks it in an envelope next to his cash register. Then he says the weirdest thing, "It's not the alcohol I have to worry about you handling here."

I have no fucking idea what he's talking about, so I

raise my glass, toasting his oddball statement and pulling a refreshing sip from my mug. The shit isn't half bad. I'm feeling better already.

· · · **XXX** · · ·

Sitting at the corner stool, enjoying my whatever-the-fuck-it-is cold beer, I notice a detail I hadn't immediately observed when I walked into this odd place. It is quiet. There aren't any TV's on, and a jukebox stands in the corner, screaming only in light and not sound. I realize this once the cold suds sink into my gut and trips my Pavlovian instinct to want to watch a baseball game on the tube or bop my head along to something from AC/DC's Back in Black album.

Chances are the Yanks are getting ready to play. Willie Randolph is probably taking B.P. while Phil Rizzuto is prattling on about where he and the grandkids went for dinner in the Hamptons over the weekend.

"Ho-lee cow!" he would be saying to Bill White who would be laughing half-heartedly at his jokes while waiting for an opening to turn the talk back to baseball and the game at hand.

"TV broken?" I call to the bartender.

He shrugs. "Might be. There's a jukebox."

I pull another gulp of beer and get up to browse the jukebox. I plunk in four quarters that are jingling around among other change in my pocket. I pick out some Hall and Oates, Men at Work, Duran Duran and, of course, Toto. I love that Africa song, it's been a constant earworm ever since I heard Casey Kasem play it on American Top 40 a few weeks ago.

The tunes start playing and it gives the empty bar some much-needed atmosphere. I saddle up at the corner stool and start swaying to Karma Chameleon. Don't judge me!

A door I didn't notice was behind opens and someone walks in. It's not the front door that I came in. It's also not either of the bathrooms that I noted were off in a hall over by the jukebox. I can't see the newcomer over my shoulder. I can swivel around but choose not to look that interested. Instead, I wait for the stranger to belly up to the bar to size them up.

· · · XXX · · ·

The guy walks past me and steps up to the bar a few stools down from my position. His shirt, a bright powder blue, features the likeness of Mr. T ironed on with his catchphrase, "I Pity the Fool". He's sporting a mustache that makes it appear like he's trying to go for the Tom Selleck look, but he looks more like the perverted weatherman on the 6 o'clock news.

He orders a drink from the bartender. The bartender shoots me a nervous look, like I know something. I don't know anything. He turns and fixes a drink for the new patron.

I sip my beer. It's getting warm. I put the rest of it back figuring I can get the bartender to give me a refill since he's in the serving mode again.

To my surprise, the bartender places the drink he just made for the new patron in front of me. "Compliments of the gentleman over there," he says, before going back to his business of wiping the inside of mugs with his towel.

I don't want to get into mixed drinks. I look over to the new guy to politely decline the drink. He's already walking over to me insisting, "drink, drink!"

He's got an accent. Something European, a bit harsh like Germanic but not as aggressive.

"Thanks very much but I'm just sticking to beer." I say to him, hoping I had spoken my protest loud enough for the bartender to hear me so he can just pour me another round of that whatever-the-fuck beer.

"No, please. Not strong." the guy says in his accent.

I surrender. But I don't take a drink. I'm hoping I can just smile nice at the guy and bail out of the bar. I didn't want to be bothered this early in the evening.

"You are new here?" he asks me.

"Yeah, well, to this place anyway. Its... different here. Do you come here often?"

"Come. Go. All the time."

This guy is really weird. He's putting me on the defensive and I'm not sure why. His abrupt answers are odd. Even for a guy who is obviously foreign.

I ask, "Are you going or coming right now?"

"Going," he says. His smile is big, a little too big, like Freddy Mercury's smile.

"Oh, well thanks for the drink then! If I see you again, the next one's on me!" I tell him hoping that he'll go wherever it is he's going to.

He reaches out and pinches the shoulder of my Members Only jacket, "You are a member, yes?" He laughs at his dumb unoriginal joke, "Members have to open the door for me, please."

He indicates the front door, the one I came in.

Now I get a bit indignant. If this guy thinks I'm his personal doorman, he's a few power pills short of a Pac-Man game. What kind of weirdo buys someone a drink just so they can get them to do their bidding?

I snicker at him, "I'm good. You've got two arms, I'm sure you can figure it out."

"Please," the guy says. He looks a bit worried now, like he is running out of sand in a cursed hourglass.

Now I'm just flat out annoyed with this guy. "Dude, you need to take a chill pill before I total you."

"Totally?" the guys asks.

"Totally." I tell him.

His eyes are darting all over the place. He wasn't expecting me to be a douche to him about opening the door. I see beads of sweat breaking out on his forehead. He is getting red hot right before my eyes.

"Dude, get away from me with your grody ass." I tell him.

He looks me in the eyes and screams like a frog in a great deal of pain.

I jump to my feet. It's time to total this jerk.

"What's your beef?" I ask him, ready for the fight.

"Where's the beef?" he asks me. It sounds rhetorical.

He runs past me and back out through the door he came in through.

I look at the bartender. He'd been watching in his peripheral vision, pretending not to see the altercation but failing in feigning his disinterest.

My gut is to blame the bartender because he's the only one left in the bar besides myself. "What the fuck was that?" I ask him. I sound more accusatory than I had intended.

"Takes diff'rent strokes," is all he offers in the way of an explanation.

It's more of an explanation than my near accusation deserved. "To rule the world," I say to him, "Sorry. Guy got under my skin."

"Well, at least you got a free drink out of it," he says, indicating the drink that fucked up guy had bought before he got all weird.

I don't want to drink it, but my heart is pounding, and I throw back a big gulp to settle my nerves. It works.

And the drink isn't half bad.

"What is that anyway?" I ask the bartender.

"It's called a Demonic Persuasion."

"That's a bad name." I tell him.

"I guess."

"No. I mean like bad meaning good."

"I may be old but I'm hip to your jive," he says and winks.

I swallow another mouthful of the Demonic Persuasion and settle back into the corner stool.

Not only is the Demonic Persuasion a good drink, it's now half gone and I'm feeling some effects. I slide it to the side and take another pull on my whatever-the-fuck beer before that gets warm like piss. Nobody likes piss-warm beer.

· · · XXX · · ·

The guy sitting at the corner stool is making the bartender nervous. He's the kind of guy that is going to make his shift a long one. The bartender just wants to fulfill his obligation to *them* and go home. Just like he has every night since January 1, 1980.

"What's brought you here, stranger?" the barkeep asks the guy sitting at the corner stool.

He didn't expect the answer, "Would you believe me if I told you gymnastics?"

"Well, I'd believe ya but I can't say that was the reason I was expecting. Usually it's about a girl. It's always about a girl."

"I'd rather not get into the specifics," the guy at the corner stool tells him.

The bartender shrugs but the fact that the guy doesn't want to open up about what sort of trouble has brought him here is troubling. Nobody comes to this bar because they are just out looking for a good time. This place just doesn't attract that type of clientele. Something about gymnastics is eating this guy up and, if he doesn't open up, the bartender is not going to be able to help him out.

And the world outside is going to be doomed, as well.

That won't affect the bartender, but he will sure be lonely.

The keep watches as the stranger at the corner stool takes another sip of the drink that Argonon bought him. Argonon didn't have much luck but you can bet he's warned at least a few of the others. The next one will be along shortly with a new tactic. The Demon Persuasion will help but the guy with gymnastics issues is pretty stoic.

Good thing, because the bartender has no idea how he's going to warn him yet.

· · · **XXX** · · ·

A bunch of minutes have passed since the jerk tried to start shit with me. The bartender is being a bit nosey but that's what bartenders do I suppose. I'm drinking my beer to maintain a light buzz. I'm feeling good. I've almost forgotten why I stopped at this bar in the first place.

I hear the door open behind me and my mood is ruined. That dickhead is back; I'm sure of it but I will not turn around. I half expect he's going to sucker punch me from behind.

Instead of getting sucker punched, I hear footsteps shuffle over to the jukebox. I glance over my shoulder. It's not the same dude. It's another dude. He looks cool. Just wearing jeans and a black t-shirt. He's even wearing those cool looking KangaROOS sneakers with the Velcro straps. Anyone wearing Velcro sneakers is okay in my book.

One of my tunes is still playing on the jukebox. I have no idea if I've got any songs left. I just hope the guy's taste in music is as good as his taste in clothes. I sip my beer and wait to hear the verdict.

I hear a succession of quarters plunk into the machine. The sound makes me hope he plays some Joan Jett. I know that song is like two years old, but it still sounds radical.

Instead of Joan Jett, Air Supply comes on. Gag me with a spoon, like, totally.

I can hear the *tap, tap, tap, tap* of the guy punching in more numbers on the jukebox to songs I'm certain I will dislike as much as Air Supply. When he's done, he sits at the bar to my left, leaving one stool between us. The guy looks at me and gives me one of those guy nods, a curt jerk of the chin in my general direction. Too cool to say hi but still civil enough to acknowledge my existence.

I guy nod back.

The bartender approaches him. The guy gives the bartender a guy nod.

The bartender guy nod's back.

We're all dudes and we've all affirmed one another's existence.

The dude orders a beer. He named one of the ones on the beer board without looking up. He's a regular.

The bartender slides a frosty mug of suds in front of the new dude with the Velcro KangaROOS and an affinity for Air Supply.

"What they got you in for?" he asks without looking at me.

"I'm a free man." I tell him. What the heck is it with everyone wondering why I'm here?

He snickers at my answer before pulling a sip off the

head of his beer. "No man is free. Especially not in this place. This is the kinda place everyone spends their entire life trying to escape from. Of course, there's always one sure way out."

I get the reference. The guy is playing the James Dean version of Piano Man. "I can walk out of here and never come back friend. I'm just passing through."

"I'd love to get out of here. Been trying to get out of here my whole life. But here I am, once again," he says toward the bottom of his glass. "Hey, I'll get the next round. You tell me how it is you get out of here so easily."

Air Supply ended. Olivia Newton-John followed. How could a guy rocking the new wave look pick out such crumby songs? I'm going to need to take this guy up on his offer just to stomach the music. Plus, I'm interested in where his line of jive is going. He's a man looking for answers. Maybe I can get some myself with a little drunken bar banter.

"Sounds good," I extend my hand over to him, "I'm Dusty."

He snickers again, taking another drink from his mug instead of returning my handshake. "Snake."

"No, I'm on the level, man." I say, jumping on the defensive against his sudden accusation.

Another snicker, "No, I'm Snake."

"Oh! Well, good to meet you Snake."

We both throw back the last of the beer in front of us.

"Whatcha drinking?" Snake asks me.

"Fucked if I know. Just give me one of whatever you're drinking."

He snickers. He throws up two fingers to the bartender. The bartender jumps into action.

"What's with these weird beers anyway?" I ask, figuring he's got the scoop on the lack of Budweiser.

Before he can answer, the opening riff to Joan Jett's "I Love Rock n' Roll" belts out of the speakers on the jukebox. Instead of answering, he holds up a finger at me like he just put the world on pause. He gets off the stool and steps back behind it assuming the air guitar stance and begins to play along.

I smile.

I get up myself as the bartender is pouring our beers behind the bar. While Snake plays on his invisible Les Paul, I begin to sing along as if I have the signature Joan Jett scratch in my voice. I don't but I'm still feeling the buzz.

On the final "Yeah, me!" Snake joins it and sings out as loud as he can. We're the only people in the bar besides the bartender so it's easier for me to let loose even with the buzz. Snake taking the lead on just rocking out also helps.

We go on like that through the first chorus and saddle back up on our stools when the bartender places two cold ones at our spots.

"I fuckin' love this song! I was hoping you were going to play it."

The oddest thing happens. Snake smiles at me and there is something very serpentine about his smile. "You were?" he asks, the python grin never breaking as he speaks.

I pause, the smile takes me off guard. "Uh, yeah. Yeah. Love Joan Jett. What gives with all the Air Supply junk though? Sounds like the kind of stuff they'd play in—"

"Hell," he finishes for me.

A tingle freezes my spine. "Yeah," I say and a nervous chuckle escapes my mouth.

"Hey. Take a pull on that beer so you can show me how you get out of here, hotshot." Snake says.

The serpent smile is gone in an instant. He's normal again just like that.

"What are you in for," I ask, "that you need to escape?"

He bites. "I've done bad things Dusty."

Jesus, I wasn't expecting this guy to tell me he's a criminal or anything like that. I'm thinking I'm going to get some sob story about a poor choice in career paths and a history of being unlucky in love that have left him stuck in the never-ending loop of living life at the local tap room.

"Having a hard time coping with that?" I ask. I've

76

crossed a few people in my time on this Earth that have done some shitty stuff and they've turned to the bottle to deal with things they've done. Beer is the cheapest therapy I know.

Snake looks at me, looks *through* me, "Yeah, hard time coping with that." His focus snaps back on my face, "Open that door for me, and I'll be able to cope much better."

"God helps those who help themselves." I say, being a bit of a wise ass.

I wasn't ready for the level of reaction my snide remark earned.

"Fine! Who needs you anyway! Go to Hell, Dusty. Go! To! Hell!"

Snake bolts up, knocking his stool over onto the floor with a bang that reverberates loudly in the mostly empty bar. He spits at my feet, turns on his heels and walks back through the door he'd come in through in the back.

Obviously, he has no trouble opening a door for himself. Jerk.

· · · **XXX** · · ·

The bartender busied himself by washing a few mugs that were clean already. He didn't want to make it obvious to the guy at the corner stool that he was trying to keep tabs on him. He didn't expect the second demon to give up that easily. There was blood in the water, however, and another would be along soon. In fact, he'd be surprised if it was only one that showed up now.

The guy had handled himself well so far. The guy didn't know he was handling himself well, but he definitely wasn't a sucker. The others were going to have to put some more work on him if they wanted to get out.

Still, there was the gymnastics thing. Dusty, as he overheard him when he introduced himself, still hadn't come clean on the gymnastics stuff. He was going to need to let that out before the ones from the other door got it out of him. Before any more showed up, the bartender tried to dig at him like toenail dirt.

"Don't let 'em get to you. The regulars tend to be a little tense around here. I can see you're kinda tense yourself. Is it that gymnastics thing?" the bartender asks Dusty.

Dusty jolts, surprised by the bartender, as if he'd forgotten he was there. "A little tense? My gymnastics issue makes me a little tense; that Snake guy is about as tense as a rubber band ready to snap."

"Gymnastics. Sounds like a sport loaded with tension if you ask me. Are you good at it?

Dusty chuckles. "Yeah, I'm good at it. A little too good."

"Oh, a rivalry is it?"

Before Dusty can answer, the back door opens. Dusty turns to look at who's coming in through the portal. The bartender curses under his breath. They are moving quick and in numbers now.

· · · XXX · · ·

I must have parked in the wrong spot. Everyone is coming in through the back door. I got nervous thinking I had really set off Snake and he was coming back in with a crowbar to take care of me.

Instead, it was a group. Like, a music group. Survivor specifically. I know because I just saw them play *Eye of the Tiger* on American Bandstand this past weekend. The first dude through the door is wearing jeans, a white shirt with black suspenders and a beret. The guy through the door behind him wears a bushy mullet and big wire-rimmed glasses. The next two guys in sport button up black shirts, one in a leather vest, the other has two thin ties around his collarless shirt. The ties are sharp.

Bringing up the rear of the fivesome is a chick. She looks good. Her hair is teased up with bangs curling like Niagara Falls over her forehead. She's wearing enough rouge to make her cheeks look like burning suns. Her delicious hips are poured into a spandex leotard and pink knit leggings.

I know they know I'm sitting here but they ignore me in a collective act of cool. Suspenders and Mullet walk over to the billiards table. Vest and Tie sit at a high top near the pool table to watch. The Olivia Newton-John look-alike saunters over to the jukebox.

My eyes are magnetized to her posterior as it sways. She leans over the jukebox far more than necessary, choosing to intoxicate me with her curves instead of worrying about bad posture. She's aware I'm leering at her. I should be worried one of the guys from Survivor is her boyfriend, but my libido is not allowing me any level of tact whatsoever.

Her ass gyrates to Hall and Oates playing at random while the jukebox awaits more coins. I'm transfixed on her ass, praying she plays "Let's Get Physical". It's an awful pop song but her posterior is built to move to that particular song.

AC/DC plays on the jukebox. The opening strums to "You Shook Me All Night Long" fill the bar. When the drum hits and the song kicks in, she spins around and moves like a stripper in front of the jukebox.

I'm sure there isn't a single pair of eyes that aren't plastered to her right now, but I don't care to glance around to confirm that and miss a single iota of her performance.

I wish for God to make a stripper pole appear out of thin air, but God isn't listening. The beauty is undulating her hips, her legs swaying like two sex-crazed snakes wrapped in knit leg warmers. Her white Reebok high-tops are a fine stand-in for 6-inch stilettos, though the latter would make this moment perfection. The kicker is watching her nipples stiffen under her tight-fitting leotard. This is turning her on as much as it is me.

I'm hypnotized until I realize she's dancing for *me*. I snap out of my libidinous gaze and squirm on my stool. As much as I enjoy watching her dance, she did come in with the group of guys and I can only assume she is attached to one of them.

I turn my head to the floor but let my eyes scan the barroom. None of the other guys are giving me the stink eye. In fact, the guys at the billiards table are too wrapped up in their game to even watch the girl dancing. The other two glance over at her but avert their attention back to the game when someone is about to take a shot.

I don't want to turn back around and face the bar. The dancer would be insulted, she's still dancing right at me. I see a sinister grin on her face. She knows I'm uncomfortable. She catches my eyes glancing up at her and pushes out her chest, making her nipples as prominent as the tips of the pool cues.

The AC/DC anthem ends, and I become aware of the fact that my forehead is covered in cold sweat. I use the break in songs to turn back to the bar. The bartender is busy washing glasses and doesn't see me wagging my finger for another round. I realize turning my back to the girl is worse. I can't see what she's doing, and it is making me that much more anxious.

I feel a gentle hand on my shoulder and a voice say, "This round is on me, Big Boy."

I nearly jizz in my pants from the sensuality that drips from the attractive vibrations of her voice. If there is a Heaven and it is populated by angels, I am certain that every one of those ethereal beings would speak with the exact inflection of my dancing beauty.

I want to say something witty. Something that will make her giggle or melt off her panties. Instead I say, "Oh, cool."

She giggles at me, "You're cute." Then to the bartender, "Two!" She makes a clicking noise at him like he's a horse that she's calling over.

The bartender shakes his head in the negative at her but doesn't look her way. I think he's joking but she gnashes her teeth together and speaks an octave lower, "Two."

I'm watching the exchange like I'm front row at the U.S. Open. My head turns back to the bartender, his play.

He closes his eyes and takes a deep breath. "As you wish," he tells her.

I get the impression they may be related. Siblings perhaps and he's looking out for his little sis.

"Little brother?" I ask.

She snickers, raises a knowing eyebrow and says nothing else.

"How about the others?" I ask, "Older brothers? Boyfriends?"

Her sly smile never disappears, "Not boyfriends, not brothers. But they do look out for me."

"Guess that makes me the lucky guy." I say, not really knowing what else to say but not wanting to lose any momentum I've gained. I worry I'm shooting myself in the foot. I'm good at doing that when it comes to the ladies.

"Luck, maybe. Cute, definitely."

"I don't need to tell you how good looking you are," I say, another failed attempt at witty banter.

"Good looking? And here I was going for slutty."

I want to tell her she is excelling at slutty. I don't. I feel like that line will backfire on me worse. The only thing I've got before my lack of retort turns into awkward silence is a nervous chuckle and a half-hearted, "Yah."

Now I wish she would pour the drink she is buying me on my face and walk away before this gets anymore awkward.

She doesn't. Instead, she lifts her glass that the obedient bartender has just placed in front of us. "To sluts," she toasts.

"To sluts!" I say picking up my glass, as well. I may not be dead in the water yet.

I sip my drink. She takes several gulps of hers.

The sip I take burns. I fight the urge to react to the unexpected amount of alcohol in the drink at the same time I fight the urge to widen my eyes in awe at her ability to drink it down like water. This girl is no lightweight and I may have gotten in over my head. And that kinda turns me on.

"How do you like?" She asks.

"Good." I answer as I feel my equilibrium begin to falter.

After all the free drinks I've had since sitting down in this bar, it's finally starting to work on my head. As strong as the alcohol in this drink is, it still shouldn't be working on me that quickly. I make a calculated decision to place the drink back on the bar and pretend it doesn't exist.

Not because I don't want to get drunk, which I do. I just don't want to get drunk while it seems I've got a legitimate shot with the foxy lady.

"Let's go pick out some more songs to play," I offer. I figure that will buy me some time away from the strong drink and a moment to walk it off a bit, while at the same time getting a new angle on my game with this girl.

She smiles and accepts but insists we take our drinks with us. I grab the glass but have zero intention of taking another sip until we browse the jukebox catalog and pick out some songs that might afford me a chance to get her moving her intoxicating hips once more. Maybe even with my hips moving along with hers.

She leads the way back over to the jukebox. I see two of her friends, the ones not playing pool, watch me out of the corner of my eye. My buzz is still strong, so I don't care when I stare at her ass as she walks. I know they don't like it and I know there isn't anything they can do about it. It's obvious she calls the shots with the other guys.

She already leaning over the jukebox, peering in its window, choosing her next song. Her ass wiggles like a serpent: slow, sexy and seductive. I hear the sound of a snake charmers flute play in my mind in time with the metronomic swaying of her posterior.

Before I can look over her shoulder and try to add my own choice to the mix, she turns and faces me. A new song has started to play. It starts soft and symphonic. I stand where I am. There is a look in her eye like she is either going to pounce on me and eat me or rip off her clothes and start dancing naked. I'm fine with either option.

The song creeps toward the melody and I recognize it once it kicks in.

Foreigner's "I've Been Waiting For A Girl Like You". More ridiculous music, but, in the moment, I'll forgive it for existing on the fringe of acceptable rock music and the fact that she's about to gyrate to it.

It's not something I even know how to dance to, but I find my shoulders begin to sway in time with her hips. She inches closer to me.

Her movement is doing little to belay my intoxication. My head is swirling into the dark shadows of the moment. My vision tunnels and in my mind only she and I exist. I step to her, place my hands on her hips. My heart burns; my fingertips tingle with jolts of electricity shooting through them, energized from the heat leaping off her body.

She pulls me to her. My arms embrace her, she embraces me. I swoon, the lyrics seem so perfect in the moment. I may mistake passion for love, but I don't care. She's making me drunker. I'll do anything for the woman just to spend every moment from here forward with her.

"Let's get out of here," she whispers in my ear.

My knees almost buckle from the implication of her suggestion. I don't want to break the embrace. I don't want to lose the moment. I don't want to leave with her just yet and I don't know how to tell her that without blowing my chance at glory.

"Okay," I whisper back into her ear.

I need to buy a little time. Just a little. If I break our dancing embrace, I'm sure I'll fall like an inebriated hobo straight to the floor. "I'd like to finish this dance though, you move so divinely."

I don't know if I sound like Casanova or an idiot. For a fleeting moment, it feels like she clenches my shoulders but relaxes again just as fast. Did my suggestion irritate her? Is she so horny that she really just wants to go now? Forget the wining and dining? Well, I guess we already covered the wining.

I cannot deny her aggressive behavior is as intimidating as being locked in a cage with a pacing tiger. There is a demon battling an angel on my shoulders and the angel is winning. I am in a predicament most men dream about and I am balking.

What is wrong with me!

Instead of asking again, she breaks our swaying embrace and grabs me by the hand. Her grip is rough, firm, like she's my mother and about to pull me away for a beating. A moment ago, I was intimidated, now I am scared.

She drags me to the door.

"Open it! Let's go!"

I don't know how I've gone from a tender moment to feeling ashamed for who knows what at her blowing her top.

I reach for the door handle but stop when I realize, once again, another patron of the bar is insisting I open the front door for them. The webs of alcohol cluttering my mind clear like a strong wind blowing through my brain.

"I don't want to leave. Not yet," I tell her.

The most fucked up thing happens at that moment. First, her eyes glow red like they're laser blasters from Star Wars about to reign hellfire upon me. Then her voice drops several octaves lower than when she had spoken before. All in all, I'd say she looked absolutely demonic in that moment.

"Open. The Fucking. Door," she says. Only, she sounds like an 80-year-old man with a five-pack-a-day habit since he was three years old.

Needless to say, at that point, I don't feel the urge to oblige her charms as much as I had moments ago. Instead, I back away from the door, holding my hands up at my sides, making it clear I am not going to take part in any door opening for the rest of the night, if not the remainder of my existence.

The idea slams me in the back of the head like a frying pan: *Not going to open that door for the remainder of my existence.* What was it that guy Snake or maybe the bartender had said to me earlier? Something about never leaving? Was I trapped here now, for eternity?

The bartender!

I look over to him. He's giving me the hard side-eye.

The girl of my dreams, on the other hand, is grunting like a bull. Her eyes continue to flame red. She snorts sulfuric smoke from her nostrils. Getting lucky with her tonight no longer seems to be an option.

I'm sure she is going to attack me. I prepare myself to see my own innards pooling in blood on the floor in front of me. I never wanted to see my intestines spool out of my stomach but I'm sure that is where this night is going.

Instead she bends over on all fours and walks canine-like over to the group she had come in with, still milling about the billiards table. Their game had stopped, a scattering of pool balls still on the table. They hadn't enough time to finish out their first game.

They weren't going to finish either. My girl, with the radiant red eyes, mounts the table on all fours. She's facing me and growling, teeth bared like an angry dog, eyes flashing at me. One of the guys mounts the table behind her. He tugs at her leotard.

They begin humping like... well, like two horny dogs. There is rhythmic humming, it's coming from everywhere and nowhere. The hum nearly drowns out the jukebox. There is something ritualistic about the whole scene.

I want to run. I know I can't. It's obvious I cannot open the front door and leave.

That's exactly what they want. It's what they've wanted all along.

I don't know why.

As my girl humps on the billiards table, her flesh starts to take on a red hue like an infection growing under her skin. The guy mounted behind her also reddens. I want to believe they are blushing from the strenuous activity they are engaged in but when steam blossoms off their bodies, I think otherwise.

I swear I can see horns budding out of her forehead as she grinds against the dude behind her. The sex looks painful. I definitely don't want to get lucky with her tonight. Or any night heretofore.

The steam around their bodies intensifies. I can barely see them behind the fog. I worry they might explode.

And then they do.

A fantastic blue ball of flames radiates outward in an instant. I am blown to the floor; the wind gets knocked out of me. My mind tells me I'm dead before my body can process the fact that, somehow, I'm not.

I lay there, looking up at the ceiling, breathing hard, trying to retake my breath. The bar is quiet, normal. I can't process it all.

I look around. The bar is fine, like nothing happened. The jukebox is playing Olivia Newton-John's *Magic*. There is nobody in the bar save for me and the bartender. He doesn't even seem to notice me lying on the beer-soaked floor on my back.

I get up and dust off. I sit back on the stool at the corner of the bar. There is a drink there waiting for me.

What the fuck?

· · · ✗✗✗ · · ·

"Bullshit!" I say to the bartender, slapping the drink like it's a bitch and deserves it. The alcohol spills all over the bar top. "What is this place? What the fuck is going on here? This ain't no bar!"

The bartender sighs. He looks like he's still trying to come up with an excuse for everything that has happened. He shakes his head, defeated.

"They want out. You want in." He tells me.

Now instead of being vague, he's being cryptic.

"What the fuck does that mean? Just level with me. What is going on here?" I beg.

"I can't say."

"What do you mean you can't say? I know damned well you know what's going on around here. You haven't flinched even once with all these lunatics coming in the back door."

A light clicks on in my head. The back door, everyone but me has come into the bar through the back door. I had assumed there was more parking around back that was the preferred entrance for regulars. Every one of them wanted me to open the front door though, the way I had come in. The only way outside I knew.

"Where does that door lead?" I asked the bartender throwing a thumb over my shoulder to the back door behind me.

"It leads in."

More of the cryptic shit again. I want to scream and wring his neck. I take a deep breath, hoping logic and reason can win the day over violence.

"It leads in to where?"

"I can't say."

I grumbled like an upset grizzly bear, on the inside. On the outside, I changed my line of questioning.

"Why can't you say? You don't know or you're not allowed to say?"

"Yeah."

"Oh God," I say, raising my voice but reeling it back into a calm demeanor, "Yes which? Yes, you don't know, or yes, you're not at liberty to say?"

He changes the line of questioning on me, "Why can't *you* talk about gymnastics?"

He deflates me in an instant, "I can't say."

Son of a bitch.

"You'd better learn how to say. I can say that."

"Why, what does it matter. How does that stop the insanity that comes through the back door? That doesn't make an iota of sense."

"The truth will set you free or you will set the truth free."

I take another deep breath. The weight was too great. This is starting to feel more like therapy than drinking away my troubles. It would be great to peel off that bandage and let the wound ooze out the infected pus trapped in my mind. But the bartender at some hole in the wall dump is not equipped to handle the truth.

How does he even know about the gymnastics stuff? Nothing had gotten out about it. Yet I got the impression that he knew more about that stuff that he was letting on. Maybe talking it out with him *could* set me free.

I need a drink.

The bartender put a fresh mug in front of me. He knew. He knows everything.

I grab the ice-cold mug and raise it in salute to the bartender. I take a swig and begin to tell him my story.

· · · **XXX** · · ·

"Gymnastics is pure hell." I begin.

He held up his hand, pausing me. Behind me, I hear the door open.

Fuck this shit. I'm nipping this asshole in the bud before he can even get started.

I stand up and turn to tell whoever walked in to get the fuck out and save everyone the trouble.

I didn't expect to come face to face with a demon.

"I'm pure hell," the demon said. He spits to the side; it singes the floorboard where it lands.

I know this demon.

"I know you," I told the demon.

"Of course, you do, Dusty."

"You are the worst scum that has ever set foot in a gymnasium anywhere and any when on this Earth, *Mary Lou Retton*."

The demon snickers.

"Oh Dusty. Let's cut the shit. Open that door for me and let's get this over with."

"Fuck. You."

I can't believe Mary Lou Retton is here. What are the odds? She has as much chance at winning a gold medal at the upcoming Olympic games as she does of me opening that front door for her.

"I'm walking out that door tonight. Then I'm going to walk down that street outside, straight to the highway and head due west to the 1984 Olympic Games."

"I told you before Mary Lou, *you* aren't good enough."

"We'll see about that!" She spits at my feet, the ground sizzles again and I can feel heat lick at my toes through my shoes.

Mary Lou Retton isn't good enough for the Olympics. She knows it. I know it. I'm her coach or... I was her coach. She didn't have the stuff. She refused to accept that fact. Instead of grasping reality and refocusing herself, she had signed a deal with the devil.

Louis C. Feir is a gymnastics coach who's despised by anyone in the business with a code of ethics. He's notorious for taking talented gymnasts, chewing them up and spitting them out. Mary Lou went to train with him when I told her I could not justify training her for the Olympic team trials.

Of course, Mary Lou won a spot on the team. When the news got out that my prodigy had won a spot on the U.S. team, I was let go. The owners at my gym were furious I had neglected to hone her talent and bring the prestige of having an Olympic gymnast that had trained at our gym.

I packed my things and walked out of that gym. And somehow, the path that started at that gymnasium had ended here at this bar. It looked like the greatest place to quietly drink away my sorrows.

Instead, it seems I walked out of one Hell and into another.

Mary Lou is a cute little kid. She's a talented gymnast. She is dedicated, a little too dedicated. It's that imbalance between talent and dedication that has gotten her into trouble. Most up and coming hopefuls have drive, like Mary Lou, but they reach that level just below the Olympic level and they realize they just don't have that extra little edge needed to put them over the top. That realization is always enough to take the wind out of the sails of dedication.

From there, most young, talented women who have aspired to be in the Olympics come to accept they won't get to the world stage. They still have extraordinary talent that they can hone and use to serve them well in other areas of gymnastics, typically coaching, at some level. This should have been Mary Lou Retton's story.

Her dedication never dwindled. She knew she wasn't good enough and she didn't care. There are rare instances, when the drive doesn't die, that a gymnast will find the extra little push and make it. A Cinderella story. But Mary Lou had found a much easier route to Los Angeles in Coach Fier.

You might say she signed a deal with the devil.

I say she let her pride get the best of her and allowed herself to be manipulated by a man who only wanted to chew her up and spit her out and take all the cash that was left in her wake.

· · · XXX · · ·

"You could have made a life for yourself," I tell Mary Lou.

"I am making a life for myself, you non-believer. I'm headed to Los Angeles no thanks to you," she tells me.

I throw my head back and laugh at her. The joke is on her. I know how this shit works. "You're not going anywhere. I know how this shit works and there ain't no way I'm going to open that door for you so you can just turn your ass around and go back where you belong."

"Open the door Coach Dusty," Mary Lou says, her voice now more human and adorable. She had shed the demonic routine like snakes shed skin.

"It's not going to work. I know what you are now. You're already gone."

"Open that door! I deserve this!" she says, the crushed gravel returning to her true voice.

I don't even bother. I turn my back on her and go back to the corner stool. Mary Lou would pitch a fit. She would carry on and throw a tantrum like a spoiled schoolgirl and go back where she came from. I had become jaded to the routine already.

You can imagine my shock when I feel my feet leave the ground as I reach my stool. Mary Lou picks me up and lifts me over her head like she's Andre the Giant. My feet flail, my hands whip around trying to find something to grab on to so I can stabilize myself. I'm looking at ceiling tiles and awaiting the inevitable slam down on the beer-soaked wood floor.

The body slam never comes. Instead I float over to the front door. Mary Lou has no intention of allowing me to refuse her demand.

"Open the door," she says and instead of a body slam onto the floor I'm slammed face first into the front door.

The cartilage in my nose cracks and I know I'll be one notch uglier for the remainder of my life. How much life I have left to live will be determined by how I navigate the next few moments.

Mary Lou keeps a firm grip on me after my intimate introduction with the door. I'm glad because I would have crumpled to the floor without her help.

She shakes me again, "Open it," she repeats.

"No," I say, my lips pressed against the door.

The demon gymnast pulls me back and slams me into the door once more. "Open," she demands.

"Nuh uh," I tell her, fighting the urge to pass out.

It's been a long time since I'd last taken a beating. I was in my early twenties, spending my weekends out at the clubs. Every now and again I would get in a brush up with some drunk dude who takes umbrage to me bumping into him or looking at his girl the wrong way or fucking his mother or some shit. I've had my fair share of lumps and bumps but none of those scraps compare to the whooping Mary Lou Retton is laying down on me.

I am hopeless to fight back. My only defense is the knowledge she can't kill me. For some dumb reason, all these fucking things that had come in the bar tonight need me to open the door for them. Not once had any of them deferred to the bartender to open the door for them and it is obvious they are not able do it themselves.

Demonic rules are so weird.

· · · **XXX** · · ·

The bartender watches Mary Lou Retton beat the shit out of Dusty. Most bartenders would shout at Mary Lou to knock it off before she broke the door and would remind her that, if she did break the door, she would be paying for it. The bartender at this bar had been through this before.

Even the times before this was a bar and before he was the bartender in the bar.

The bartender had been here since the gates of hell were first opened at this portal. There are, of course, portals from Hell all over the Earth. This one is his to guard. The bartender isn't a demon; he's a gatekeeper. He is a sort of lost soul and a servant to the demons. He does as he's told, for all of time and then some.

He is never to interfere.

So, he watches as the demon known as Mary Lou Retton pummels Dusty to within inches of his death. She will not kill him, not if she wants out. That's the thing about the portal from Hell. Demons can't just walk on to the Earth. They must be invited. It's an odd formality but it all plays to the magics at work, facilitating a demon's ability to walk the realm Earth exists within.

It's true, a demon can take the possession route and inhabit an Earthly vessel, but that method has its limitations. The preferred method is to roam the Earth in pure demonic form. No limitations and freedom unlike that in their hellish existence. A vacation for demon-kind.

The bartender's impressed with Dusty's wherewithal. It's been quite some time since the demons had to try this hard. It's rare they show themselves for what they are, using out and out fear to get their way. Most times all it takes is a drink or two. Maybe flash some cash or tits depending on the human target and away they went.

Dusty had a defense. He was a gymnastics coach. No demon could have seen that coming. The bartender knew it right away. It's the chalk. The chalk gives it away every time. Gymnastics coaches and pool sharks are always coated in chalk. The way of the world only a former human like the bartender could have keyed in to.

Dusty could have talked about it. He could have opened up about Mary Lou and the shortcuts and his integrity as a coach and love of the sport. The bartender could have told him it was time to go, before the demons showed up and played their little game. It should never have been Dusty at the corner stool. He had too much fight left in him. He would not crumble like any plain, old drunk, the usual candidate to sit on the corner stool.

The bartender felt bad. It shouldn't be Dusty and he knew it. But he couldn't break his vow, his oath to the netherworld.

Could he?

Is there a way he could justify the redemption of Dusty the gymnastics coach? Could he save him from the very demon who his student had sold her soul to? There would be poetic justice to it all, but blood-thirsty demons weren't ones for romanticism.

Could he betray the demons without them knowing? It is risky. If he gets caught, he could be erased. It would be a fate worse than death. But he isn't a demon and right is right.

The bartender pours a shot.

· · · **XXX** · · ·

"Wait," I hear the bartender say, "let the guy have a drink before he dies."

What a swell guy, I think to myself. But since he flat out tells me that I'm about to be killed by this demon, which is the opposite of how I saw this going, I figure I wouldn't mind a shot after all. I hope it's something good and strong.

The demon pulls me up off the floor and, instead of slamming my face into the door once more, she opts to have my face meet the top of the bar. I don't know if it's all the head trauma I've suffered already but the wood on the bar top feels softer. I'll take any bright side I can get at this moment. I thank God I am still coherent enough to have that insane thought.

I'm kind of glad she plans to kill me. I'm already picturing the astronomical doctor bills I'll be racking up with all the visits to various neuro-specialists that will have to treat me from the vicious concussions I've already suffered.

My thoughts are all over the place. My thoughts don't make sense at the moment. The shot in front of my face looks like medicine. I want to drink it. It will make me better, mommy.

Mary Lou lifts my head off the bar by my beautiful mane of hair. I think some comes out, my scalp burns. Maybe it's my brains. Ouch.

"Drink," Mary Lou Retton tells me.

I snicker. It's funny that she thinks she has to instruct

me. She is the one controlling my limp body now. I'm a demon's puppet.

"Shove your hand up my ass," I tell her and laugh. I'm losing my marbles.

Somewhere deep inside I'm coherent enough to understand the rest of me has gone bye-bye. My mind checking out before my body has the chance. This is what it must feel like when a puppet dies, I thought.

I wish for a hand up my ass. It will fill me with life.

I don't get a hand up my ass. I'm being manipulated more like a ventriloquist's dummy. My head is being yanked by the hair on the back of my head. Another hand opens my mouth. And then the shot goes in.

I remember stories about 'the cocktail' you get when they strap you down to execute you by lethal injection. This is the cocktail, I assure myself.

I don't want to die but at least I stood by my britches and refused to open the door for Mary Lou Retton and her cadre of demons from Hell. She won't get to the Olympics after all. She had sold her soul for nothing. Ha!

I feel the drink fill my mouth and I allow it down the back of my throat. It burns like tequila but tastes like nothing.

I hear the jukebox change songs. A guitar plays a catchy little riff. It's twangy sounding, gritty and dirty. It sounds like music that belongs in a bar. A drum crashes and bangs to punctuate the riff and then kicks into gear.

I recognize it right away. AC/DC's *Have A Drink on Me*.

I don't know if it's the shot or the song, but I feel the strength fire back into my bones, spread out into my muscles and explode in my nerves. I feel great!

I shrug off Mary Lou like I'm a big burly bouncer. I feel surreal. Then, I roar and spit fire. I mean, I literally spit fire.

Bad ass!

I hiss red hot lightning at Mary Lou. Her leg catches fire and she shrieks. Her skin melts like the witch in the Wizard of Oz, reduced to a smoldering pile of nothing in a matter of moments.

Mary Lou curses. Her skin and muscle burnt down to her bone, but she still stands on her charred leg bone. Instead of attacking me, she leaps over the bar and goes for the bartender. I'm not expecting that. What the hell did he do to her?

I don't interfere. I watch, kind of entertained and curious. The bartender has been a total dick to me thus far; I think he's earned this beating. Not sure if it is justified as much as karma catching up to him.

I stand and watch, fixated as the demon lays into the bartender. Mary Lou is really letting him have it. That must be what I looked like a few minutes ago.

That's when it strikes me. A few minutes ago, I was about to breath my last breath. In a matter of moments, I'm rejuvenated. Right after I took that shot. The one the bartender had poured for me. He had saved my ass.

Son of a bitch! I must return the favor.

· · · **XXX** · · ·

The bartender is taking a beating. He deserves it. He had broken the code. His actions had jeopardized the portal. The punishment, worse than death: annihilation. Complete and painful erasure from existence, his mark on the cosmos erased. His effect on time and space rendered null and void.

But first he had to experience extreme pain. Demonic torture is horrible if you're already a lost soul. But, if you aren't a soul yet, it's something worse. You can't die but you are also physically incapable of coping with the level of pain a demon can inflict. Souls are designed to be tortured for eternities. Flesh and bone, not so much.

Humans that experience extreme pain have a defense mechanism known as shock. But those are biological mechanisms developed over millennia to deal with pain that could be felt in the physical plain. The equivalent of shock a soul experiences cannot carry over into the physical being.

But it doesn't mean death. It means experiencing a

level of pain your brain cannot comprehend; therefore, it cannot go into shock and protect you from processing that hellish sensation you are experiencing. It is worse than being driven mad. Your brain literally fries itself from the sensory overload.

Demons love torturing flesh and bone beings for that very reason. There is a satisfaction in it they can never achieve while torturing the souls of the damned in Hell. Mary Lou Retton is really getting her rocks off beating the bartender for his transgressions against demon-kind.

It's better than the Olympics, at least for the demon inside of her. But her sold-out soul is still fresh, and the human still left dying inside of her somewhere desires her moment of glory in the Olympics. And so, there is a certain restraint in the beating she's delivering. A human would never see her pulling her punches though because they are still more brutal than a human eye is capable of processing with the naked eye.

The bartender, knowing full well what he was doing when he did it, had slipped Dusty a drink that would help his mind understand the severity of the situation. That and the superhuman power he'd also been infused with to stand up to the demons, if only for a few moments.

It was still a gamble. He had placed his bet on Dusty knowing what to do with that power when he realized he had it.

· · · **XXX** · · ·

Popeye comes to my mind. I feel just like Popeye. In fact, I feel so much like Popeye that I roll up my sleeve, hoping to find an absurdly bloated bicep emblazoned with a fully animated tattoo of a battleship blasting its guns in a glorious burst of flame and smoke. My bicep is just a bicep though.

That doesn't matter, because I still *feel* like my bicep has the power of the navy's ultimate weapon on the seven seas. Whatever the bartender had slipped me in that shot is making me feel like Superman.

I reach over the bar and grab Mary Lou by the back of the neck, as she beats the shit out of the bartender. Before I can pound her head into the bar, she does a standing backflip and twists her way out of my grip. At least the bartender is getting a moment of reprieve.

I won't worry about him. I pivot and keep focus on Mary Lou Retton. She completes a double backflip over the bar. Most would be in awe of her gymnastic ability but not me. This is standard stuff she's pulling. A double backflip isn't going to get you a spot on the U.S. Olympic Gymnastics team. I can handle her if she is going to keep coming at me with this entry-level shit.

I vault over the bar top like I had just hit the pommel horse. No big feat for me either, especially with the shot of vigor the bartender had slipped me.

Mary Lou cartwheels at me, attempting to make herself a human (or demonic) Chinese throwing star. I parry by leaping into a somersault forty-five degrees left of her forward assault. I dodge another attack.

We can do this dance all night. I know she knows she's got to put a bit of distance between her and me to attempt anything that could catch me off guard. She needs a vicious floor exercise-like combo I won't be ready for. I'm ready for anything she brings my way. I trained her.

There is an X-factor. I don't know what the demon, Coach Lou C. Feir, has taught her. My gamble is nothing. Coach Feir is known for cutting corners. He'd rather manipulate, intimidate and influence outside forces than put in the hard work and push Mary Lou to a level she is physically incapable of achieving.

That's to my advantage. Just because she hasn't been trained to Olympic standards doesn't mean I haven't.

I don't have the advantage of having a set of rings nearby. But there are two fans dangling far enough down from the tall ceiling I estimate can accomplish what I need them to before Mary Lou can charge me again. I leap up and I grab hold of two of them. It's an awkward grip, nothing at all like the ergonomic grip the rings provide but I won't be up here doing an entire routine.

I swivel my hips back and forth, kicking forward and back, gaining momentum. Mary Lou gets an idea of what I'm trying to do and charges to stop my momentum before I can build up to full force.

I throw all my weight into the pendulum my body is creating. I need a full rotation before she is on me. There isn't much room and I strain my hips to bring me around full swing like a Ferris wheel.

I hear her scream, giving everything she has to reach me. The muscles in my hips scream as I push myself over the top. Full rotation. My feet meet Mary Lou's face like a battering ram. She's launched backward off her feet with tremendous force.

I don't realize how much vigor the bartender's shot has provided me. I don't expect to launch Mary Lou off her feet, let alone launch her like a ball bearing out of a slingshot.

I should have felt the pride of victory in that moment, like knowing you are getting perfect 10's before the scores are flashed on the big board. To my horror, my gold medal moment on the ceiling fans is turned into a moment of horror as I watch Mary Lou Retton rocket across the bar directly at the front door.

· · · **XXX** · · ·

The bartender polishes an already dry glass with his well-worn bar towel. The bar is dead. He hates to busy himself with boondoggle work but he's happy to still have a job. The one that got away, got away in a most fortuitous way.

He was able to work the loopholes in the demonic rules. Technically, it was Dusty that let the demon out. *Technically*. There was no tribunal, no instant replay or slow-motion captures from three different angles of the events of that night. There was his version of the story and nobody to dispute it. Nobody knew about the shot.

The bartender might have avoided losing his job but the punishment for what he had done that night may have been much worse. He was stuck with Dusty until Dusty figured out the only door out was the one the demons walked through. That was the price. One demon let loose into the world to be paid for with one human soul joining the circles of Hell through the back door.

Like the front door stuff, Dusty must figure it out for himself. And he is slow on putting the pieces together. Or maybe he isn't. He'd sat around the bar for weeks now, nursing beer after beer. He's now a fixture just like the stools and the billiards table and the jukebox.

There he sits, quiet, at the corner stool, sipping beer he still doesn't know the name of and listening to songs you aren't meant to dance to. He says it is the best spot in the bar.

··· **XXX** ···

"Corner stool," I say, raising another frosty mug of whatever-the-fuck name the bartender had given the beer this week.

"Best spot in the bar," the bartender finishes for me.

I've said it enough, it's become my tagline, almost like when that cute little kid on Diff'rnt Strokes would say, "Whatchu' talkin' 'bout Willis?"

I've been sitting here at the corner stool for almost two months since the Mary Lou thing. I'm depressed. I'd let her get away. Not just the whole demon thing, but Mary Lou herself. She was going to be able to compete in the Olympics.

I watch the news every night. I pay special attention to all the Olympic coverage once it starts. The women's gymnastics event is going to be the highlight of the entire games. Not only are the games in Los Angeles this year, the U.S. women's team is expected to be competitive. The buzz is they can place very high in the competition because the eastern European teams that dominated the sport are boycotting the games taking place in the United States.

I know better. It's more demonic influence on behalf of the demon known as Mary Lou Retton, alongside her coach, Lou C. Feir.

She had made my life a living Hell. I know now what the demon, who called himself Snake, had meant when he said people never left the bar. I know the score. One demon out and one human in. I'm pretty sure the bartender thinks I'm too stupid to realize how this thing plays out. The fact of the matter is I'm not walking through the back door until I watch the Olympics.

I'm obsessed with Mary Lou as much as Mary Lou is obsessed with the Olympics.

"Turn on the TV, it's time."

The prime-time Olympic coverage started. The bar began to fill with the evening's regulars. The crowd is a little more robust that usual; no doubt several folks want to head out to the bar for a few drinks while they watch the much-hyped U.S. women's team compete for the gold on their home turf. Everyone knew the potential for an unforgettable moment in American sports history being made tonight.

I have the best seat in the house, the corner stool. It doesn't matter how crowded the bar is, you can see the TV and everything else from this spot. So, I have an unobstructed view as Mary Lou Retton steps up the vault.

The gold is almost locked. Mary Lou will have to score a perfect 10 on the vault in order to win it. Unheard of, even for a demon. She has two vaults, but the chances of getting a perfect score are against her.

I'll revel in this moment. The last shred of satisfaction I will have over Mary Lou. She will not get her gold metal after all. I'm all smiles.

I hold my breath as Mary Lou salutes the judge and begins her charge toward the vault beam. Just before she hits the springboard, I hear the TV commentator say, "Ugh," disappointed. She screwed up, the perfect score evaporated. Redemption.

An instant later she hits the springboard, bounds off the beam, twisted in the air and lands on the mat like it's coated with Krazy glue.

Impossible!

It looks like the perfect vault. The bar erupts in cheers. Mary Lou's vault looked picture perfect.

The air is electric in the bar as the world waits for the judges' scores.

10. A perfect 10.

She had done the impossible. An inhuman feat when the chips were stacked against her. If I owned a gun, I would have blown my brains out right there. How can the world not see she is an inhuman devil who had sold her soul for fame and fortune?

The people in the bar are celebrating as if *they* had all just won the gold medal.

Mary Lou, being the fucking shitty show-off that she is, is entitled to a second vault even though it's completely unnecessary. And you know what?

She does a *second* perfect 10 vault.

Hello! As if one was impossible, back to back perfect 10's is unimaginable. Your chances of hitting the lottery twice are greater.

Nobody questions it. They believe she is that good. They don't know. I do.

I get up off the corner stool, dig into my pocket and leave the bartender his tip.

We look at each other for a moment through the sea of celebrating fools. He nods at me. I shrug. He knows I know.

I turn around and open the door to Hell.

Time for another fool to enter the front door. First drink will be on me.

THE LAST TAPROOM ON THE EDGE OF THE WORLD

(III)

PAUL PULLED THE car into the cemetery and drove up the small hill. Nolan watched as the headstones and extravagant grave-markers passed by. The storm was still in full-force, assaulting the road and the windshield, making it almost impossible to see into the distance. Lightning crashed and lit up the place, and Nolan shrank in his seat, second-guessing his decision to come along. Between the weather and the story Paul McDaniel had just relayed in the words of an old gymnastics coach, Nolan wasn't really *feeling* the situation.

"Why are we here?" Nolan asked, as Paul whipped around the bend, probably too fast for these terrible driving conditions.

"Told you," he said. "We've come to visit my friend."

"He's dead?"

"Of course, he's dead." Paul chuckled. "Haven't you been listening to a goddamn thing I said?"

"So, the door? It really did lead to Hell?"

"You know, for a writer, you really are a few breadsticks short of a basket."

Nolan rubbed his eyes. Between the beers and the tales, his brain was on the verge of shutting down. Right now, he wanted to climb into bed, drift off into a dreamless sleep. He doubted his next snooze would be dreamless considering the thoughts and projected images Paul's stories had given him.

No. There will be horror. Monsters. Demons. Ghosts.

"I think we should head back. It's getting late and I have a hell of a headache. We can resume this—"

"Nonsense. You came here for your story, so a story is what you're gonna get." Paul didn't seem interested in slowing down. Heading back. Stopping with the tales. He seemed intent on driving through the maddening storm, risking both their lives. And for what? To prove what he'd said was true? Didn't matter whose name was on that headstone, it wouldn't prove a goddamn thing.

Nolan thought about opening the door, diving out. He'd seen it in the movies, and it didn't look all that hard. Worst-case-scenario, at this speed, he'd only break a bone or two. Might be worth it considering he was driving with an absolute nut-job.

"The coach's grave is just up ahead. Hold onto your horses." He said this as if he knew Nolan was getting antsy, contemplating an early exit.

Paul drove a little farther, taking the bends at a speed Nolan wasn't all that comfortable with. When he located the desired grave, he pulled over, onto the grass, dangerously close to a random headstone, so close that Nolan believed the tire would roll right over it. He thought his position was disrespectful to the dead, but he didn't say a word. At this point, he figured he'd go with the flow, not raise any concerns, and ride out the night.

How bad could it get? It wasn't like he was in danger. If it did come down to it, he could always take the old man in a fight. He wasn't a brawler—never had been—but, if he felt his life was at risk, then he'd be ready to throw down. He didn't have that feeling now, and, though he wasn't sure how the night would end, he was positive the old man meant him no harm. He was a little crazy, a little eccentric, sure, but not dangerous.

He's an old man for Christ's sakes. Just a lonely old man.

"Here we go," Paul said, looking over at him.

Nolan nodded. A few seconds of silence passed between them. Paul raised his eyebrows as if he were waiting for Nolan to make his move.

"Wait," Nolan said, jerking his thumb toward the window. "You don't expect me to get out in this, do you?"

"Of course."

"For what reason?"

Paul pinched the bridge of his nose. "Jesus Flipping Christ. You sure are short on brains, ain't'cha."

"I guess so. I don't follow. At all."

"Just get out of the goddamn car."

"It's pouring out there."

"It's water. Not acid. You'll be fine."

Paul opened his door, stepped out, rounded his vehicle and popped the trunk.

This guy's nuts. Absolutely bonkers. I should have stayed home tonight. Continued my research on the Internet. Not have come out here. I should have—

His car door opened. The sound of rain crashing down around him filled his ears.

Paul shouted, "Let's go! Quicker you get out here, quicker we can move on from this place!"

The old man had two shovels in his hand.

Oh fuck no. FUCK NO.

"I don't think we should—"

Paul grabbed Nolan by his collar and ripped him out of his seat, dragging him into the wet atmosphere.

"What the fuck, man!" The old dude had a lot of strength for someone who looked so brittle. He'd lifted Nolan up from his seat as if he were a child. As if he weighed almost nothing.

Paul handed him a shovel. "Let's go. Won't take long. We didn't bury him that deep." He started walking toward the row of small headstones.

At first, Nolan didn't follow. Didn't want to. He thought about letting the old man lead himself out there, then taking his car. Driving back to the bar. Getting in his own car and driving back to the city. Leaving this nightmare behind. Fuck Paul McDaniel. He could walk back for all he cared, rain or no rain.

Paul shouted over the rainfall. "You even think about leaving me behind, you'll be one sorry son of a bitch!"

Gooseflesh danced over his skin, his scalp alive with a million invisible night-crawlers.

After that, Nolan decided he wouldn't try anything like that. He wouldn't try to escape unless Paul tried to do something to him. Tried to...

...kill me?

He was certain it wouldn't come to that.

Wasn't he?

Paul started to dig. Nolan came up behind him, looked at the small plot of land before the headstone with Coach Dusty's name on it. He couldn't read the last name because it had been marked up, scratched and weathered down. He barely made out the name *Dusty*.

Nolan sunk his shovel into the dirt. Dug. Took them twenty minutes, twenty minutes of strenuous labor, but finally, they hit wood.

A casket.

Did he take me all the way out here just to see a dead body?

It didn't make sense. But, then again, Paul *had* said he wanted to see his old friend again. Nolan just had no idea he had meant *this*.

They cleared the dirt around the casket, enough so they could open it. The old man knelt in the wet dirt, reached down and undid the latches on the side. He opened the casket like a guitar case, revealing the thing that lay inside.

Nothing.

Empty.

What the shit?

Nolan opened his mouth to speak, but his voice had abandoned him.

"Dusty, Dusty, Dusty," Paul said. "You old son of a bitch, you."

"Where's the body?" Nolan asked over the downpour. Even if he'd died in the eighties, there should have been a skeleton or something.

"If I had to guess... somewhere in the deepest depths of Hell."

Nolan laughed incredulously. "Come on, man. This has gone on far enough." He had had enough of the funny man and his funny games. It was time to go home now. Time to leave and forget he ever met Paul McDaniel.

The man is a kook.

"You don't believe?"

Nolan shook his head, his longish hair sending droplets airborne. "No. This is madness."

"Madness, yes. Madness is correct." He climbed out of the shallow grave. With Nolan's help, he pulled himself up from the dirt pad and onto his feet.

"You're insane. You realize that?"

"Am I?" Paul flashed him a smile just as lightning lit up the cemetery. It sent shivers down Nolan's back. "You haven't seen anything out of the ordinary on this very night?"

Nolan tried his best, but he couldn't block out the image of the girl. She'd come to him while he was in the bathroom, back at the Ocean View Hotel. Covered in blood. Speaking silently.

Warning me, he thought. *Warning me to stay away from Paul McDaniel.*

"No, nothing."

"No?" Paul glared at him, as if he were peering inside him, having a glance at his soul. "You can't conceal the truth from me, Mr. Nolan. I'm like a hound when it comes to lies. Can smell them coming from miles away."

Nolan turned back toward the car. His shirt and pants were soaked, shoes waterlogged. It was like walking through the muddy marsh.

"Where are you going, Mr. Nolan? You cannot hide from the truth!"

Nolan pointed to the car. "I want you to take me back right now!"

Paul reared back his head and cackled at the sky. "There is no going back. Not tonight." He picked up the closest shovel, started tossing dirt over the empty casket. "Come. Help. I have one more story to share and then we'll be done with this... madness, as you call it. Then you can decide what is real and what is not."

Nolan opened his mouth, fully planning to tell the old man to fuck himself, but he stopped himself. He had come this far. He didn't have his car with him. Paul was his ride, and, whether he liked it or not, he was stranded here. Hadn't the slightest clue where he was or how to get home. He considered his options and decided being stuck in the middle of the cemetery in an unfamiliar town, this close to midnight and caught in the storm's worst, wasn't the road he wanted to take.

Dragging himself back over to the open grave, he cursed himself for being such an idiot.

The royalties on this fucking book better be worth it.

"One more story, huh?" Nolan said, picking up the other shovel.

"Oh yeah. This one is killer, I promise. Your fans will love it."

Fans? He wasn't aware he had many of those, even though his readings packed in a fairly decent crowd.

"Lay it on me, I guess," he said, as if there were another option.

Paul heaved another shovel's worth on the wooden box. "It was the nineties," he said. "The spot that was once called Bayberry Bluff was then abandoned, a scrap heap that sat in the center of town."

"What happened to the previous owners?"

"Disappeared, if you can believe it. I'd already left by that time. Went to Germany for three years in the late eighties to work for a world-renowned brewmaster. When I came back, Bayberry Bluff was in ruin. For some legal reason, the town couldn't demolish the site. So, instead, they tried to sell it."

"Who would buy that place?"

"That, my friend, is what this next tale is all about..." Paul smiled devilishly one more time, so wide that Nolan saw more teeth than face, and the rainfall continued its attack on the harrowing night.

ALTERNATIVE

WHILE ALLI ONLY saw a decrepit building, fallen into ruin after sitting vacant for five years, Jackson saw a real estate steal.

"It has good bones," Jackson had said for the fifth time today. It was his go-to mantra and one he firmly believed in. He'd been searching the city for the perfect place to start his brewery, and when the realtor, Miss Smoltz, had said the building had, at several times in its illustrious past, already been a bar, restaurant and brewery, Jackson knew this was the right place. "I feel really positive about it."

Alli shook her head. She was staring up at the second-floor dirty windows, despite the cold rain pelting their faces. "There's something wrong here. Tragic, even. So much loss."

Jackson turned her face away, to pull her from her negative shit and to save her from droning on and on about her stupid visions and premonitions.

He knew she was a psychic. Card and palm reader. She's picked up the bullshit from her mother, who'd learned it from her mom and so on. Gypsies, tramps and thieves in her family. Jackson loved her to death, and she was awesome to be around. He was even thinking about popping the Question once the brewery was making even a small profit, but her witchcraft garbage was getting on his nerves lately.

Jackson was under enough stress. He didn't need her tossing around her opinion about each location as if it was going to be part of his final decision. It had been a mistake having her come on these showings, and he thought once they were done and he was making his final run through the three possibilities she'd stay home. Hang out with her odd family. Go find a few friends.

Be somewhere else so Jackson didn't have to get pissed because she was ruining his buzz. His positive energy.

"Let's go inside." Jackson had the keys in hand and jingled them with a smile, hoping Alli would at least smile.

Not a chance. She crossed her arms and went back to staring at the upper windows. "You're making a big mistake. One I can't be a part of."

"What do you mean?" Jackson knew exactly what she meant because she'd been hinting at leaving him all week. She'd been subtle at first, treating him like a child. Commenting about the other properties and how she could really see them working. Ignoring this building at first, until it was obvious Jackson was more interested in it.

He felt drawn to it, as strongly as she was repulsed. Jackson knew this was coming. He silently joked she wasn't the only fortuneteller in the relationship.

Former relationship? When she refused to answer his question, Jackson smiled. He loved her. He wanted a life together. Babies. A white picket fence and a dog and cat. "Why don't we meet back up tonight at seven? The Marina Diner? I'll even let you order the eighteen-dollar salad with shrimp and won't make fun of you. Fair?"

He stopped smiling when he saw the look on Alli's face.

"No. I can't be a part of this... this," Alli said and shook her hand at the building. "Nothing good will come of it. I'm begging you to buy one of the other buildings. Please, Jackson. I'll even throw in ten thousand dollars."

"Ten thousand dollars?"

Alli sighed. "Fine. Twenty but it's all I have in savings."

"I thought you had nothing in savings, actually." Jackson felt betrayed and annoyed. "When did you suddenly come into money?"

Alli sighed. "My mother. I talked to her..."

"No fucking way." Jackson was waving his hands. His face felt red with anger. "This is all me. No loans from family. I didn't ask my parents for a fucking dime."

Alli smiled but it was more out of pity than happy. "Your parents don't have any money."

"Fuck you," Jackson said automatically. She'd never thrown it in his face before. "I won't take a penny from your mother. Her cash was earned by bilking weak people into thinking they were talking to grandpa in Heaven or some other bullshit. She's a con artist. Her money is shit because she stole it from stupid people."

"Is that what you think I do?" Alli asked.

Jackson opened his mouth to speak but shut it. He didn't want to fight with her. He loved Alli, but lately she was so negative. Especially when it came to real estate. Was she jealous of him? She'd never owned anything in her life. Alli had to travel all over the country with her gypsy mother, the snake oil salesman. He was sure after a few weeks or months of her stealing money from gullible people she was always shown as the fraud she was, and it was time to move on to the next town.

"Fine." Alli put her head down. "I'm leaving. Don't call me ever again." She took three steps back before lifting her head, but it wasn't to look at Jackson. She was staring at the upper windows again.

· · · **XXX** · · ·

Jackson had managed to scrub another layer of caked-in dirt and beer remnants from the bar and smiled. "Look at this history."

"More like dried puke and beer," his brother Trevor said. He didn't look happy. "Can we take a break? We've been at this for hours."

Jackson checked his watch. "Actually, about an hour. You're a lazy bastard."

Trevor waved his hand dismissively. "I'm turning on the radio."

"Sounds good. It's too quiet in here, anyway." Jackson

went back to work on the bar, marveling at the natural wood finish underneath the grime. There were indented circles where hundreds, maybe thousands, of beers had sat. Condensation rings that would never go away and he didn't want them to. Small chips from the wood where he imagined nervous patrons had picked at it while trying to pick up a woman or man.

He moved a foot to his right and frowned, running a finger over the three deep grooves in the wood. "What do you think this is?"

Trevor was too busy trying to find a station on the small radio Jackson had purchased. "I think this thing is busted. All I get is static and weird noises. You hear that?"

Jackson stopped looking at the bar and frowned again. "Is that... a child laughing? That shit is creepy. Find a different station."

"That's just it... I can't lock onto anything except the laughing. It's so faint, too. Even when I crank the volume, it doesn't get any louder." Trevor turned off the radio. "I hope you kept your receipt. I'll bring my CD player tomorrow and we'll have some real tunes. The radio sucks anyway."

"Very true, but none of that alternative shit you're listening to. Bring in some cool eighties stuff. I don't care if it's even heavy or not, I hate Pearl Jam and Nirvana and that junk," Jackson said. His brother was only eighteen months younger, but they were worlds apart when it came to music, vices and women.

Jackson was into heavy metal and hard rock, but he hated the ballads. He liked loud guitars. Trevor was more into whining singers who hated their parents, and grunge had struck a chord with him.

An occasional drink and a cigar, once a month or so, was enough to loosen up Jackson and he had a good time. He was a happy drunk; although, it was rare he had anything other than a good buzz. Trevor was a heavy drinker who was never finished until he passed out. Until he dropped, he'd get to the point where he was an asshole, saying whatever was on his mind.

Women was where they were really different, though. Jackson was always the knight in shining armor. He'd find broken girls and try to fix them. At least, that's what his therapist said. He thought he was simply looking for love but, after the divorce of his parents when he was ten, he'd been changed. As stupid as that sounded to Jackson, he knew it was true. He had abandonment issues with women. His parents were absent from his life. When he'd been unable to go to college because he had no money and his parents both made too much for him to get grants but wouldn't spare a dime to help him, he'd gone into construction. He'd dated quite a few gorgeous women over the years but nothing as serious as Alli.

"Tonight, I got a hot date," Trevor said. "I need to skip out by five and take care of a couple things."

Trevor was the guy whose friends said would fuck a snake. He only had one type: vagina. Their friends loved taking Trevor barhopping because he'd fall on the grenade for them, hitting on and usually sleeping with the fat friend or the ugly friend or running interference with whichever girl they didn't want cock-blocking. As far as Jackson knew, his brother had never been in a relationship longer than two weeks.

"We're just getting started," Jackson said. "I could really use you to help me clean the rest of this room. Did you see the mess in the storeroom? I need to hire a crew to clear it."

"Then hire professionals."

Jackson shook his head. "What I mean by a crew is the guys coming over and drinking a case or two of beer and renting a dumpster. I'm barely hanging on with this right now. I need to get it ready for inspection and open the doors before end of year or I'm dead."

Trevor smiled. "Ask Alli if she'll give you the money."

"Fuck you, asshole," Jackson said and shook his head with a smile. "You can be a real jerkoff. You know?"

"Oh, I know. It's a gift." Trevor wiped the sweat from his face. "Come out with me tonight. I met a stripper."

"Of course, you did."

Trevor laughed. "What do strippers have?"

"Stripper friends."

Trevor snapped. "Exactly. This one's a little chubby, which I love. She thinks she's not good enough. She'll do just about anything."

Jackson sighed. "You've been with her already?"

"Nope. I just know the look." Trevor pointed at his crotch. "Make sure you shave your bush down, too. Stripper chicks love dudes who shave their balls."

Jackson shook his head. "I don't think so. That shit itches for weeks."

"Not if you keep it shaved."

Jackson put his head down with a laugh and went back to cleaning the bar.

"Seriously, dude, you need a break occasionally. All this stress is going to kill you, big brother."

· · · **XXX** · · ·

Jackson felt bad for blowing off his brother, but he needed to keep pace, or the brewery was never going to open on time. He had deliveries of equipment coming in four weeks. With all his cash tied up in the building and incoming items, Jackson couldn't buy a beer tonight anyway.

He needed to finish the bar area tonight and then go home and take a power nap. Return at first light and tackle the bathroom. The plumbing was still intact, and he crossed his fingers everything still worked. If replacing more than the toilets and sinks was an issue, he was fucked right now.

With no construction work in his immediate future, it had been the perfect time to start the work on the building. Of course, without a paycheck, it meant his meager savings were going to dry up quickly.

Jackson didn't tell Trevor, but he'd been surviving on a can of tuna and tap water for meals for the past three days. He needed to strip down everything to make the brewery a success.

He'd sold his record collection and his PlayStation and

games, as well as books, extra clothing and anything not bolted down, at a yard sale last weekend. All the hardcover and paperback books he'd collected over the years he was never going to read.

All that work for a few hundred dollars, when he could've thrown it all in the garbage and gotten a jump on cleaning the building.

Something heavy fell in the stockroom, the noise in the silence sounding like an explosion. Jackson had been reaching across the bar for a clean rag when it happened and slipped, hitting his chin on the edge of the bar and seeing stars.

He was on his knees and feeling nauseous. *Fucking idiot. The brewery is going to kill me yet.*

Jackson stood and got his bearings, shaking it off.

There were no further noises from the stockroom, but he knew he had to investigate. He felt so alone in the building right now, in the industrial part of town where everyone else on the block went home at five o'clock. Except for the vermin, Jackson was by himself. He had a really bad feeling in the pit of his stomach.

"Anyone there?" Jackson sighed. It was the line everyone used in every bad eighty's horror movie. The serial killer never answered but they knew where the victim was now.

Jackson picked up a hammer and screwdriver from the nearest toolbox and went to the stockroom door. He'd kept all the lights off in the building to save money, using only a couple of lamps he moved from spot to spot as he worked.

Now he flipped every light switch on the wall and the bar area was bathed in harsh light. Most of the bulbs above were yellow and gave off a sickly light.

"I'm coming in," Jackson announced, the worst possible thing to do. He pushed the stockroom door open with his foot and held the hammer cocked and ready to strike.

The stockroom was a mess and, with the lights on, it looked even worse.

He heard scurrying but it was probably a few mice and cockroaches running from the light.

The path through the stockroom was thin, barely enough room to walk single-file. Jackson had walked through a couple of times to the back door and the small dumpster in the fenced-in pen outside. The realtor had apologized for the mess and all the debris, but swore the seller was knocking the price down so they didn't have to clean it. There was also talk of actual, working equipment buried in the trash, too. Jackson knew every little bit helped. His shoestring budget didn't allow him to pay more for the place so they would clean it out.

Beggars can't be choosers, he thought.

He looked around but couldn't find anything even more out of place than before. Something heavy had fallen but there was nothing in the path. The same wall of junk on either side looked undisturbed. Jackson sighed. It would take a week with a dozen guys to clear this out.

The focus was still on the main room, especially past the bar area where the actual equipment would be set up and the beer made. Jackson envisioned a viewing area, where customers could sit facing the kettles and watch workers brewing beer, packaging bottles and cans and filling the kegs. Fresh beer for the masses.

Jackson turned back. He'd figure out what had fallen in the future. Right now, he needed to finish cleaning the bar.

The woman was beautiful. An older redhead. Wearing tight jeans and a tighter t-shirt with the name of a bar, Lost Demon Brewing Company. She was staring at the floor where Jackson was standing. He followed her gaze and jumped back, crashing into boxes.

A blood-covered tarp was on the floor. He could smell the coppery stench and his stomach roiled. When he looked up, the redhead was gone.

The blood and the tarp were gone, replaced by the dusty floor and his footprints.

· · · **XXX** · · ·

"How was your night?" Jackson asked, not hiding his big grin.

"Fuck off." Trevor stared at the bar area and nodded. "You did a lot of work, bro. Did you sleep here last night?"

"Maybe." Jackson pointed at the windows. "I'd like to work on those today. I thought they were painted over but it's just grime. All they need is a good cleaning."

"Just replace them," Trevor said. "Go buy new panes and glass and we'll install them."

"First off you can't do the work. You suck at construction." Jackson pointed at his brother's face. "Second... are you going to tell me what happened to your face?"

"No big deal. I ran into a fist. The stripper had a boyfriend, and, when she found out I'd fucked her friend in her ass in the bathroom at the club while I was waiting for her shift to end, she was kinda pissed." Trevor shrugged. "Sometimes being a lover instead of a fighter has its downside."

"One guy did that to you?"

Trevor shook his head and winced. "Nah. He's also friends with the bouncers, who tipped him off I was there to pick her up. I threw a lot of punches. My knuckles and arms hurt more than my face." Trevor pointed at Jackson. "I know your bruised chin had nothing to do with a chick, unless Alli came back and popped you one. Please tell me that happened."

"Nah. I had a fight with the bar counter and it won." Jackson thought of the strange shit from last night. It all seemed like a dream now, though. Had any of it happened? He doubted it. He'd been working too many hours without sleep. Eating the bare minimum. Stress levels through the roof. He needed a good night's sleep... which he'd get in several months when everything was in order. Maybe he'd seen the redhead in the grocery store at some point and his lack of sleep had popped her into his thoughts.

Trevor picked up two of the rags and a bucket. He took a couple of steps and looked at Jackson. "Why are all the lights on?"

"Huh?" Jackson realized he'd never turned them off after last night. He'd been on edge, waiting for more sounds from the stockroom or the redhead to reappear.

He didn't want to be in the dark with only a single lamp for light. "Forgot to turn them off."

"You never put them all on. You yelled at me six times for doing it."

"At least ten before you finally stopped." Jackson went to the door for the stockroom and switched them all off except for the one over the bar. "If you can scrape all the shit off the windows, I won't need to use the lamps except at night."

Trevor nodded. "Can I ask you a question and I want an honest answer?"

"Shoot."

Trevor cocked his head to the side. "Are you broke?"

"What? No," Jackson said defensively. "Just being smart with my money."

"Bullshit. You're broke. I see the tuna cans in the garbage. Every day. Refusing to go out to lunch or dinner. No hanging in the bar with me, blowing off steam."

Jackson pointed at Trevor's face. "No thanks to getting my ass kicked with you in a strip club."

"You sunk every dime into this place. I know it. If I had money, I'd help," Trevor said. He waved his hand. "You don't have to pay me."

"No way. I promised you some cash and you'll get it. I'm not going to screw over the only family that still matters to me," Jackson said.

"Oh, you'll pay me back." Trevor smiled. "By giving me a job once this shithole is ready to go. I'll pitch in and help out for no pay. You hold onto your cash. Use it to buy an actual meal once in a while."

"I can't do that."

"You can and you will." Trevor grinned. "I have a few odd jobs coming up for a friend. I'll make more than enough money. Hell, if I make enough, I might buy into this money pit and then you can't fire me when I fuck all the bartenders on the pool table."

"Good luck. I'm only hiring dudes."

· · · **XXX** · · ·

Trevor stared at the wall and frowned. "Yo, bro… bring me the lamp. I think I found something weird."

He'd been washing down the layers of grime from the walls after he'd finished the windows, which had taken him most of the day. It was nearing midnight and Trevor knew he should've quit hours ago but he wanted to keep pace with his big brother.

What he had thought was simply part of the wall was a door set into the wall. No door frame. No knob. If he hadn't tilted his head a certain way, he wouldn't have noticed the thin seam going around.

"Whatcha got?" Jackson plugged in the lamp closer to the wall and had his flashlight out, which Trevor took.

"Lookit this…" Trevor traced the door's end with the light. "What's on the other side?"

"The stockroom."

Trevor thought it odd there'd been a door on this wall that was closed up, especially when there was the stockroom door maybe ten feet to the right.

Jackson traced it with a finger. "Maybe it's where the old door used to be? They might've added the other one because it was in a better area or they had something against this wall. I remember reading about the building in the library and I know they had a big jukebox somewhere. Haven't found actual pictures yet but I know this has been a few bars and breweries over the last hundred years or so. Maybe that's it?"

"Easy enough to find out." Trevor went into the stockroom and began pushing the junk off to the side, guessing where the door would be. When he noticed Jackson wasn't with him, he called out.

"Yeah?"

Trevor smiled. "You're not interested in this mystery?"

Jackson nodded. He looked uncomfortable and he'd turned on the lights but still had the flashlight, which he was using to shine into the dark corners of the large room. "It's creepy back here."

"You notice anything odd about this building?" Trevor asked.

"Besides the creep factor I just mentioned?"

Trevor stopped digging through the trash to make a path. "No spiders. No ants. No bugs at all."

"I thought I heard mice last night," Jackson said.

"I've yet to find droppings. Mice shit all the time. Dirty little fuckers." Trevor grabbed a broken shelf and tossed it deeper into the room. "You know, if this gets rolling, and we can clean out this room, you'd be able to store a shit-ton of beer to sell. The rollup doors would need to be replaced, too, but that's an easy fix. Then you can have a fleet of trucks, in and out, delivering Trevor Beer to the Tri-State area."

"Trevor Beer? That's funny." Jackson had already had the logo designed for the place and he knew a guy who could do the sign once he got the money. Jersey Jackson Brewing was going to be huge. "Did you know one of the old businesses in this place was called Lost Demon Brewing?"

"Cool name." Trevor pushed more stuff out of the way. "I got this, by the way. I don't need your fucking help, bro."

"Not giving it so that worked out." Jackson was still shining the light around and it was starting to annoy Trevor.

"Here we go," Trevor said and pulled a rotting wooden shelving unit from the wall. It wasn't nailed to the wall, which made it easy. The wood crumbled in his hands.

There was nothing on the wall. No door on this side. Trevor rapped his knuckles on it.

"Well?" Jackson asked.

Trevor turned to his brother and frowned. "Nothing."

"Maybe they put sheetrock over where it is."

"I don't think so," Trevor said. He turned back and tapped on the wall as far in either direction as he could. "Doesn't sound any different. This wall is pretty thin, too. No way they added another layer. The wall, itself, doesn't look any different. I doubt they added a different sheetrock covering. It's all uniformly old and dirty. This is weird."

"Something else weird about this place," Jackson said quietly.

Trevor heard him but was too busy moving more shit to get further down the wall. He kept tapping every few inches but there was no change in the sound.

"Give it a rest. It's late. Let's clean up and I'll meet you back in the morning," Jackson said. "I'll even splurge and pick up a dozen donuts."

"Actual donuts? Like... Dunkin Donuts? And a large coffee, too?"

Jackson shrugged. "Sure. Why not."

Trevor laughed. "What the fuck have you done with my real brother and can you make sure he stays away?"

· · · **XXX** · · ·

It was still dark when Trevor came back. He'd been unable to sleep and, when he finally fell out, he'd had nightmares he couldn't remember details of but knew they were bad. He'd taken a quick shower, since he'd apparently ben sweating despite the cool October air, and decided to get a jump on work.

Besides... he needed to figure out why there was a door and where it went. Before they'd left a few hours ago, Trevor had told Jackson he wanted to start in the stockroom and clean it up. Start filling the small dumpster out back until they could arrange for an industrial one to be delivered. Hire a crew.

Trevor could get it done but then Jackson would ask too many questions. The guy he'd been working with doing odd jobs was Connected. A Made Man in New Jersey. He worked for The Family, and, even though Trevor knew hooking up with mobsters was a bad move in life, the money was too good. He could now brush aside his worries by knowing he'd still have enough in savings to work with his big brother for free. Everyone was a winner.

Except when he'd mentioned the building to his connection, who'd frowned and put an arm around Trevor's neck. "Never mention that place again to me. Never around anyone associated with me. You got it?"

Trevor had gotten it even if he didn't understand it.

He might be dumb, but he wasn't stupid. He'd never talk about it around anyone even remotely connected to The Family.

There were still enough guys looking for work and needing cash he'd have no problem getting a few guys together to help. Trevor smiled. He'd do well for Jackson. He wanted to see his big brother succeed. They'd had a shitty life so far. Maybe not as bad as crack houses and people being killed in front of them bad, but still worse than most. Shitty parents and shitty upbringings. It would be nice to get ahead for once.

Make a real mark in the world. The first step was Jackson's brewery.

After an hour of moving shit around and trying to make a dent in the piles of old newspapers, busted and rusting beer kegs and machine parts that looked ancient, Trevor gave up for the night.

There was always tomorrow to deal with this mess.

Right now, he needed to make a delivery and get some more cash in his pocket.

· · · XXX · · ·

Jackson had only been upstairs once, when the realtor had taken him on the initial tour. It had been clean and boring, so they hadn't spent much time on the second floor.

There were six rooms and a bathroom, and all opened onto the hallway. Each room had an identical window looking out to the street and a closet. As you came up the stairs, the wall to your left was a solid sheet without windows; although, faint markings on the wall itself left Jackson to believe years ago posters or paintings had been decorating the space.

He ran a hand over the wall and felt small grooves where the holes for pictures had been painted over. Maybe he'd have the brewery logo put into a mural on the wall.

Jackson's original excitement about the building wasn't just about the brewery downstairs. He could eventually fix up the six rooms and create apartments or rooms for rent. It would be another way to generate income.

One of the other buildings he'd look at had a similar setup and Alli had been excited about the possibility of rentals. She would've loved the idea Jackson was going to do it sometime down the line.

He missed Alli. Despite some of the fights and her mother's interference in her life, Jackson held out hope she'd come back. Maybe when the brewery was open and they had the grand opening. Jackson would make sure to get word to her somehow, so she'd know he'd done it.

In the meantime, he needed to double-check all the rooms. He didn't know why. Unlike downstairs, these rooms looked like they'd been built ten years ago instead of a hundred and ten like downstairs.

Even though the rooms were bare of furniture or even blinds on the windows, Jackson went room by room, checking behind the door and opening the closets.

He slipped into the bathroom and frowned. The toilet bowl had a nasty ring in it from lack of flushing. For now, he'd dump bleach into it and hope for the best. If he wanted to have tenants, he'd need to replace it.

As he turned to leave and go back downstairs, he stopped and opened the medicine cabinet. At first it was stuck, as if lack of use had rusted the hinges.

It popped loose like it had been vacuum sealed.

A slip of paper fell and landed on the floor before Jackson could catch it.

Jackson's mind screamed for him to run and never look back. He'd seen how this worked in every horror movie Trevor had made them watch as kids, and it never ended well.

It was either a curse on whoever found the letter or a clue to find a dead body. A serial killer confession. A black and white photo of a creepy child with long, stringy hair.

The paper had fallen in such a way only the blank back was visible.

Jackson walked out of the room. He realized he'd been holding his breath.

Run. Run.

He thought of Alli and her fear of the building. Had she been right? Maybe all the hocus pocus bullshit her family did wasn't all nonsense. Maybe she could really see or hear something wrong with the place. Feel the evil. She'd been staring at the upper level when she'd been spooked. Jackson couldn't remember if she was looking at the bathroom window or another room.

It didn't matter. She was frightened. Did he believe in her gypsy shit now?

Jackson shook his head. Fuck all that noise. He was a grown man.

He took a deep breath, walked back into the room and knelt down next to the piece of white paper, yellowed and soft on the edges. Maybe it was the deed to the entire block. A copy of the Declaration of Independence.

Jackson fought his hand to move and turn over the paper.

He gingerly gripped it with two fingers and flipped it over, jumping up and back like it was a snake.

"What the fuck..." Jackson knelt back down to inspect the writing.

It was old. Not ancient. But a few decades, he guessed.

Jackson began reading it and smiled.

It was a beer recipe for a company called Bayberry Bluff.

He thought he remembered the name as one of the original bars or breweries in this location.

Jackson picked it up and got excited. He'd found the recipe for the first beer he'd brew when they opened. He just needed to do some research and make sure no one owned the copyright or trademark or whatever it was.

· · · **XXX** · · ·

Trevor stood in the back parking lot of the building and smiled at the ten-day laborers he'd offered work to today. "Like I said... if my brother asks, you're doing this because you know me and you're getting paid in beer."

"But you're giving us cash. Right?"

"Yes. Everyone gets a hundred bucks at the end of the day. Plus, lunch on me," Trevor said.

One of the men, an older guy with a scraggly goatee and shaved head, stepped forward. "And beer. Right?"

Trevor smiled. "Of course. If there was no beer how else would you get paid? I appreciate it. We'll make two piles out here. As you bring shit out, I'll point. Really simple. The goal is to get everything out of the stockroom before night." He clapped his hands. "I have a dumpster coming. I'll buy beer and subs for lunch. Let's get to work."

"What's going on?" Jackson asked, coming outside. "Who are these guys?" He lowered his voice. "I can't pay them."

"Relax, bro. I got it covered. They're friends. I'm buying them lunch and beer. They'll have the backroom cleaned out in a couple of hours. Maybe three. Then they can help with the shit in the basement." Trevor tried to act casual, but he knew Jackson could usually see through his bullshit. "I worked this morning. Did a delivery for a friend and got paid."

Jackson looked pissed. He hooked Trevor by the arm and pulled him off to the side. "Please tell me you're not mixed up with the fucking mobster guys again?"

"No," Trevor lied. "It's legit. A guy who delivers bread and donuts into Brooklyn had a driver sick. Called me up and paid me in cash to do him the favor." Trevor grinned. "If he keeps asking me to do it, I might need to get my CDL license. The money is unreal. You shoulda bought the building for a bakery, bro."

Jackson was staring hard at Trevor and it was all he could do not to look away, a definite tell he was lying. "You're not telling me something."

"You're right... I got half a dozen donuts with the idea to share with you. I ate them all."

Jackson was still staring. He finally smiled. "I appreciate the help but keep track of every dime you spend. I will pay you back. I promise. I'm going to the bank in a few days to try to secure another loan. I have an idea." He held up a folded sheet on yellowed paper in his hand. "This could be the key. Bring back some nostalgia for the place. The new and the old kinda shit."

Trevor took the paper and read it. He nodded. "Sweet. A fucking recipe for beer. Add it to the collection. Right? Like grandpa's illegal hooch he used to make."

Their grandpa used to make his own alcohol. Moonshine. Various beers. Personal use amounts of whiskey or bourbon. The crazy bastard had grown weed in his bedroom. He was a hipster before they had a word for it, making his own drink and smoke under the radar. Trevor knew he'd learned some of the techniques while he was in prison for a few years, too.

"I think tonight I'll actually leave at a decent time and see if I can replicate this. It sounds interesting. Some odd ingredients in it, too." Jackson took the paper back, folded it and stuck it in his wallet. "What are you going to work on besides being a supervisor for your new crew?"

Trevor grinned. "I want to find out what the fuck is with the door. There's no way it leads into the stockroom. But it is a fucking door. What do you think it could be?"

"Nothing. It maybe was a door, but they sealed it up."

Trevor shook his head. "Then why not pull the door from the wall? And why no doorknob? They camouflaged it into the wall. It makes no sense."

"We have more pressing things to do," Jackson said.

Trevor shrugged. "Fine. I'll work on it after five tonight. I'm off the clock."

"You're wasting your time but good luck. I hope you find the secret," Jackson said.

"Oh, and I'll be running late tomorrow. Have another delivery to do. Won't be too late, though," Trevor said. "Depending on how much these guys get done today we might ask them to come back tomorrow."

"I can't expect these guys to work for lunch and beer," Jackson said.

Trevor waved his hand. "Nah. They owe me a few favors. It wipes the slate clean. Besides, there's no other way for you to get this much labor this cheap. Leave everything to me. Maybe make a list of what needs to be done, too. Some of these guys might have some other skills like electrician."

"We need an actual electrician for the inspection. I can't have anyone doing it."

"Sure, you can. You're in construction. You know how to cut some corners." Trevor smiled. "Might be a plumber in there, too. God knows they show enough ass crack when they work."

· · · XXX · · ·

Jackson made a batch of Bayberry Bluff and loved it. It was delicious. He'd automatically picked up his phone to call Alli but realized that ship had sailed weeks ago. He tried his brother but there was no answer.

He had a ton of work to do at the building in the morning but wanted to go to the library and use their computers to do some more research. He was sure he'd heard of Bayberry Bluff before, when he'd initially been interested in buying the place.

Jackson turned on the TV and sipped on the beer for a while, but he couldn't concentrate. He had to start on the common area past the bar, where the pool tables and dart boards would be. Eventually, when he got the money, he'd add a few TVs to the four corners so customers could watch the Yankees and Mets in the summer. Jets and Giants in the Fall. He envisioned people arguing and cheering over the Devils, Rangers and Islanders. The Knicks and Nets.

Hell, Jackson could even get some Pay-Per-Views like WWE and boxing, something to draw in the crowds and sell the beer.

Jackson finished the last drop of beer in his mug and stood. He was feeling really good. He knew he was too wound up to sleep tonight. He went into the kitchen and poured the rest of the beer he'd made into a travel container, took down one of his plastic mugs from the cabinet, found his jeans wadded up in the corner of his bedroom and his sneakers, got dressed and went back to the building.

It was quiet inside. He immediately turned on every light, knowing he was being ridiculous.

Setting the beer on the counter, he filled the mug with beer and took another generous sip. It had warmed up a bit more, but it was still delicious.

Jackson needed to scrub the grime off the walls and see what was underneath. He thought it would be wood paneling like they'd used in the 70's. That would have to be pulled down and the walls repainted or something,

More money to spend, he thought and took another sip. He knew, if he finished all the beer, he'd need to get some coffee and a power nap before he could drive home. Maybe he'd buy a cheap bed or futon and set up a room upstairs.

Jackson smiled. Why was he paying so much rent for an apartment when he could live here? He'd need to look into the laws, but he was sure he could set up residence. What else were the rooms upstairs for?

Trevor could stay, too. It would be like old times except without their horrible parents. They might be able to better reconnect. Even though they'd always stayed in touch and had gone through periods where they hung out a lot, Jackson didn't really know Trevor. He was mysterious and aloof. He never talked about his work, which Jackson knew wasn't exactly legal all the time.

Then the other rooms could be rented out and eventually Jackson would have enough money coming in from the rentals, the bar sales, distribution and beer sales, as well as private events, he could afford a new place away from work. He knew being upstairs long-term was a bad idea. He'd need some space from work, especially if he wanted an actual life.

Maybe he'd be able to show Alli how well he was doing, and she'd want to date again. If he lived at the bar, he knew she'd never agree to talk.

One thing at a time, Jackson thought and chugged more beer.

He wandered around the rooms, envisioning where the

pool table would go. Speakers for music. TV placement. One thing Jackson hadn't done yet was do this. He thought it would jinx him. He'd purposely kept in the moment when he was in the building, when it came to the bar area, but now he let his mind wander.

Explore the possibilities. Get excited for the rooms crowded with people, watching as the workers made the beer on the other side of the wall or played pool. Everyone drinking and having a great time.

Jackson tipped the container to pour more beer. It was empty. He'd finished it and felt lightheaded and tipsy. And damn good. He went to the radio and turned it on but all he got was static. Not a single station would come in. He'd forgotten to take it back to the store and either get it replaced or his money back.

He turned it off and took two steps before it suddenly began playing music.

Jackson smiled. It was the song "Heaven" by the 80's band Warrant, one of his favorites. Despite real music of the 80's now drowned out in the dark and self-absorbed music of the 90's, it was good to hear a good song somehow get past the awful stuff radio played these days.

He began to sing along, loudly, miming the moves he remembered from the video. This was real music to Jackson. Not the crap Trevor listened to, with the singer ignoring the crowd and the guitarist with his back to...

The redhead was back, standing in the stockroom. She still wore the tight jeans and the Lost Demon Brewery shirt. The overhead light made her hair glow, but Jackson couldn't see through her. She was real. Solid.

Most of the junk had been removed from the stockroom and she stood in the very center, right near the spot where she'd stood the last time he'd seen her.

"Hi," Jackson said.

She smiled.

Jackson didn't know what to say or do. He could ask her what the fuck she was doing in his building and where she'd gone the last time... Jackson looked down at her feet. There was no bloody tarp on the floor.

He also noticed she had left no footprints in the dust and dirt not yet swept up by Trevor's crew. "Who are you?"

"I'm Tina," she said quietly, which sounded way too loud to Jackson, who wasn't expecting her to speak. He thought she was a ghost, or he was hallucinating. His drunken stress-filled mind fucking with him.

She took a step forward and her eyes were locked on his. She put a hand in her back pocket and the other touched her neck.

"What do you want?" Jackson asked. "Why are you here? Are you real? Where did you go the other night?"

Tina chuckled and the sound was real and sent shivers through Jackson. She was beautiful. He'd never realized until this moment how attractive an older woman could be. The things she could teach him in bed.

"None of that matters now, Jackson," Tina said, unbuttoning her jeans but keeping them on. She knelt on the floor and pulled off her t-shirt. She wasn't wearing a bra and her full tits bounced once before settling. She dropped onto all fours. "I want you to get behind me and do me doggystyle. Slide my jeans and panties off slowly. Savor the moment."

Jackson was hard. His head was swimming with more than just alcohol. He felt... fear.

The tarp was underneath Tina. Not bloody, but he knew it would be soon enough.

Jackson turned to run out of the stockroom, out of the building, never to return to this haunted place, but instead he ran straight into the wall and knocked himself out.

· · · XXX · · ·

A screwdriver head wouldn't fit in the crack between the door and the wall. Trevor could see the thin line where they met but, no matter how small a tool he used, he couldn't wedge it in.

"How's it going?" Jackson asked, coming down the stairs. "You're in early."

"I needed to figure out this door. Didn't sleep last night." Trevor glanced at Jackson. "Looks like you didn't, either. You slept here?"

Jackson nodded and pointed up. "On the floor. I don't suggest it."

"Next time I'm out I'll find a cheap couch or a futon. We can use it to crash if we work late," Trevor said.

"That's what I'm thinking." Jackson leaned against the bar. "I need coffee."

"So do I." Trevor also needed a break from fighting this door problem. He'd done a delivery in Spanish Harlem last night but knew he was too wired to sleep, and the door was bothering him. He'd come straight to work and had finished his coffee hours ago. He took out his wallet. "Grab a couple dozen donuts, too. The crew is coming back at nine to get the last of the stockroom cleaned out and start on the basement."

"I got it," Jackson said.

Trevor smiled.

"Shut up. I'm trying not to be a cheap fuck." Jackson grinned. "I appreciate you kicking in, too. I won't forget any of this. I swear."

Trevor squinted. "Holy shit, bro, is that a bruise on your face?"

Jackson turned away. "I walked into the wall with the lights out last night. Another thing I don't suggest."

"You're shitting me."

Jackson shook his head. "I wish." He was smiling and his face was red from blushing. The bruise started at his forehead and worked down his right side to his jawline. "Can you bring back aspirin with the coffee, too?"

Trevor shook his head. "I buy means you fly, bro."

"You're right." Jackson looked wiped out. "Be back soon."

Trevor knew from the look on Jackson's face, not to mention the bruise, something else had happened. His brother would tell him when he was ready. Maybe it was Alli and she really had punched him in the face. Trevor smiled. How funny would that be? Alli was awesome but really weird. Trevor knew she didn't like him. At all. She'd commented about his bad aura and he'd made fun of her, which didn't endear him to her even further.

Some chicks are too smart for their own good, Trevor thought.

His initial idea, when Jackson had left, was to go out back and smoke a cigarette, but he knew Jackson would be pissed he'd started up again. These late-night deliveries meant he needed lots of coffee to stay awake and smoking to give him something to do while waiting for the job to be completed.

Besides, he needed to open this fucking door. Its position made no sense. He'd even had the sheetrock on the other side, in the stockroom, damaged on purpose. He'd blame one of the workers if Jackson asked and he'd hire a guy today to come in and fix it.

There was nothing odd on the other side and definitely no doorway. It looked like there'd never been one, either.

Trevor decided to bust down the doorway on this side and see what happened. He'd fix it. The guy he hired to do the sheetrock on the other side could bring two sheets. It couldn't be that hard to figure out.

He selected the biggest sledgehammer from the massive amount of tools Jackson had in the office behind the bar, where they were currently storing anything of value or anything they'd need.

"See ya later, asshole door," Trevor said with a grin and lifted the hammer over his shoulder. As a kid, he'd read a comic book, *Thor*, and he'd pretend he was the superhero, using anything he could find to use as his magical hammer.

Channeling his childhood comic book hero, Trevor took a swing and connected... with nothing. The hammer and his arm went through the wall and doorway without touching it.

He felt heat on his hands and arm and pulled back. His skin was hot to the touch, like he'd been in the sun all day or under a heat lamp.

Trevor put his hand back out and touched the cool surface of the door. "What the fuck?"

Had he imagined it? A hallucination? Did he do a shroom last night and forgotten about it?

Trevor slapped the wall. It was solid and real.

He looked at his hand and arm, which had a slight suntan to it.

"Oh, shit," he said. The sledgehammer was gone. He spun around but it was missing. Had he dropped it? Trevor went around the corner into the stockroom and laughed.

The sledgehammer was on the floor.

He grabbed it and jumped back. The metal was so hot it left a mark on his palm.

"This is some crazy shit." Trevor was excited now. It made no sense. He went to the bathroom and filled a bucket with water, going back to the stockroom and dumping some of it on the sledgehammer, which steamed the air with the heat coming off it.

Satisfied he'd cooled it down enough, Trevor lifted the hammer and went back into the other room. He hefted the hammer, still a bit warm, and struck it again.

His momentum carried not only his arm with the hammer into the door but his head and shoulders.

Trevor held his breath when the noxious stench assailed him.

It was dark but there was a soft red-orange glow in the distance. He felt a massive amount of space, like he was in the bottom of a canyon.

The heat wasn't unbearable, but it felt like he was under the direct sun in Arizona in the middle of July, yet he couldn't see an actual sun in the darkness.

"Hello?" Trevor said, and his words were flat. No echo like you'd expect in a canyon or a big space. "What the fuck is this place?"

A darker red object appeared on the horizon, moving at a fast clip.

Trevor watched as it grew in size and felt an anger emanating from it.

He decided he'd had enough and tried to pull back into the building, but he felt a grip on his shoulders. Whatever the fuck it was approaching was somehow holding him in place.

It was... a demon? *No fucking way*, thought Trevor. *This is an illusion. I'm high again and on a bad trip.*

It was red with darker crimson splotches, nearly eight feet tall, with three massive horns on its head and large, floppy ears. Three rows of teeth. Three eyes. Naked with a huge member between its legs. It stopped ten feet from Trevor and grinned through thin lips.

Trevor freaked out and tossed the hammer at it.

He closed his eyes, telling himself this wasn't real, and fought mentally and physically to escape, but he couldn't budge.

You are mine.

"Fuck you," Trevor yelled. "I want out of here."

The heat went away, cool air rushing onto his warm body. Trevor opened his eyes.

He was back in the stockroom.

"I need to buy Jackson a new sledgehammer," he thought before running out the door and puking on the sidewalk.

· · · **XXX** · · ·

Jackson kept glancing into the stockroom as he worked, expecting to see Tina again. He'd freaked out when she'd gotten down on all fours and invited him to fuck her.

It was too surreal.

Even as drunk as he was, he knew he hadn't imagined it. She was real... in a strange way he couldn't figure out. He'd watched enough horror movies to know she wasn't the nice girl from next door and was either a ghost or a monster. He pictured her mouth hinging back like an alligator and biting him in half.

Trevor had been really quiet when Jackson had returned. He'd gotten sick on the sidewalk and had to use a few buckets of water to wash it into the gutter, leaving a stench.

"You giving up on the magic door?" Jackson asked with a smile.

Trevor didn't return the smile, looking annoyed. "It's not a door. Leave it alone. We need to redo the wall and add another layer... for soundproofing. I'll hire someone to help me do it."

"You suck at construction shit."

Trevor grunted. "I said I'll fucking do it and I'll fucking do it. Back the fuck off."

Jackson threw up his hands and nodded. "My bad."

After another hour of neither really working, even when the cleanup crew arrived, Jackson decided he needed to go to the library. He'd looked into the stockroom about fifty times already, looking for Tina.

He didn't want to leave. Not with all these guys hanging around. What if she showed up and one of them fucked her?

You're the biggest asshole... what about Alli? Jackson shook his head. How soon he'd forgotten about what was probably the true love of his life. None of this would mean anything if he couldn't get her back. He'd given Alli space, hoping she'd come around and see how he was doing. At least a phone call to check in. Something.

Jackson sat down at a computer terminal at the library and began using Ask Jeeves to search for the history of the building, if there was anything online to find.

After an hour and finding only a few mentions of Bayberry Bluff and Lost Demon brewing companies, he switched to HotBot for the searches.

Jackson found quite a few pages, a couple being police reports. Missing persons. An apparent murder. No, wait. Two murders twenty years apart. At one point, the owner of the building had tried to burn it to the ground and had failed. He disappeared. When it was abandoned a few times over the decades, it had become a squatters retreat, Satanic rituals had been performed, and, for a brief period, a crack house.

The most disturbing was the fact it had been an insane asylum at the turn of the century. Countless patients had died. There was an article about a forced closing when doctors were arrested for experimenting illegally on patients and nurses for selling body parts to the local universities.

"This is all horror movie shit," Jackson said too loudly, and the librarian at her desk frowned and shook a finger at him.

Sorry, he mouthed and went back to researching. In the past few days, since working in the building, he'd thought about horror movie tropes. They were happening all around him.

Jackson read more news articles and blog posts about paranormal groups, in and out of the building, talking about ghosts and restless souls.

One article talked about a ghost-hunting team, filming a documentary, disappearing. The footage was found but no one had ever seen it; although, a snippet was given to a family member and in the article the question is posed: who was Tina and what did she do with my Billy?

Jackson froze. Tina? No way was that a coincidence; although, there was no more information. It was a copied article posted in a forum and not all of it was available.

He copied down what little information there was and rubbed his eyes. He'd been on the computer for hours, having to give up the spot every hour and put his name down for when another was available. Jackson tried using the card catalog and the reference books, but he wasn't much of a student back in the day. Microfiche was alien, too.

"Sir, we're closing. We reopen at nine," the librarian told Jackson, who had a dozen pages with scribbled notes but nothing solid. A lot of names and former businesses that meant nothing to him. He'd found a list of the owners of the property, but nothing jumped out at him.

He worried it had been a dead end and he'd lost a day of getting the brewery up to par. He needed to open as soon as possible and stop bleeding cash, even with Trevor chipping in and saving the day each day this week.

Jackson was hungry but he took the long way home, passing by Alli's apartment building. It looked like her light was out. Was she not home? Had she gone to visit her mother? Was she on a date already?

He punched the wheel in frustration. What if he went to her door and left a note? Maybe went home and called her, leaving a message on her machine? Just check in. See how she's doing.

The last place he wanted to go tonight was the building. Not at night and not alone. He'd get up early, get coffee and donuts and be in before Trevor.

Jackson thought of Tina, on all fours, and he got hard.

· · · **XXX** · · ·

This should've been another delivery. In and out. Easy as shit. Trevor had done what he'd done every other time: pulled up, parked his car and took a walk.

An hour later he came back, expecting the packages to be gone from the false bottom in the trunk and an envelope of cash under his front seat.

He'd driven for ten minutes before pulling over and reaching under the seat. No envelope stuffed with twenties and hundreds.

"Fuck me," Trevor said and got out, popping the trunk. The packages were gone. He'd been fucked over. "No fucking way."

He drove home like a maniac, lucky not to have gotten pulled over by a cop this late at night. As soon as he went inside, he knew something was wrong.

A shadow moved in the corner. Trevor hit the light switch, but the light didn't come on.

"I unscrewed the bulb. It's more private this way," a voice said. Not the shadow he'd seen, either. There was more than one person in his apartment. "Trevor, we need to talk."

"Uh... sure." Trevor stayed where he was, in reach of the door. He was trying to act casual, but his heart was hammering in his chest. He decided to speak first so there was no mistaking what had happened. "I parked the car like always. Took a walk. Came back and the packages were gone but there wasn't any money for me."

"You looked in the trunk even though you've been told time and again not to."

137

This is bullshit. "I was confused. I never look in the packages. I don't even handle them. The guy who does it, whatever the fuck his name is, does all that in the car. I just drive. I'm loyal. I've been loyal, too."

"It seems you and two other drivers have been stealing from The Family. We can't have that. The other two have already been taken care of," the voice said. "You understand, of course, this isn't personal."

Trevor was pissed. He'd been set up. No way had two other guys stolen money. He knew all three of them were getting bumped for someone else. "Who's taking over? That's really what this is about."

"I am," the shadow said and moved to Trevor, inches away and pressing Trevor against the door. "If you turn around and go quietly, it won't hurt. If you fight me, I'll make it hurt for a long time."

Trevor didn't see the blade, but he knew it was in the man's hand.

"Fine. Just make it quick," Trevor said and turned slowly around. "You both suck, just so you know."

The man chuckled, which is what Trevor was hoping.

Trevor turned and grabbed at where the hand with the blade should be, found it, and turned the wrist, plunging the knife into the man's gut.

"Fuck you, asshole," Trevor whispered as he took control of the blade and dropped to his knees, plunging the blade over and over into the man's crotch and stomach.

As the man groaned in pain, Trevor saw around the guy, just as he fell forward into the door, the other man fired two shots. They were both high, where Trevor should be standing, illuminating the room.

Trevor now had the dead man on him, but, before pushing him off, he frantically went through his pockets and found his weapon.

"You're making a big mistake. We'll be back," the man yelled, and Trevor heard glass shatter.

Trevor pushed the dead man off and fired two shots toward the window, hearing a groan as the man dove through the shattered glass.

He ran to the window, but the man was running off into the darkness, a trail of blood behind.

I'm a dead man, Trevor said. He went to the kitchen and found his flashlight.

The guy against the door he didn't recognize. He was a bloody mess, the door covered in his blood, as well as the rugs. Trevor wasn't getting his deposit back when he left.

He needed to pull this body away from the door and flee, but something caught his eye: three envelopes on his kitchen table. He opened them and shined the light on money banded in thousand-dollar blocks.

Lots of them in all three envelopes.

Trevor figured, since he was going to be a dead man soon, he might as well take the money and run. But to where?

If he left the city and tried to get out of the country, The Family would put a price on his head. He'd be a fugitive forever. He also didn't want to abandon his brother.

Then it hit him like a ton of bricks and Trevor smiled.

· · · **XXX** · · ·

Jackson set down the coffee and donuts on the bar and went around turning on the lights. It had become a habit now, even though he knew Trevor was going to comment about it when he arrived. A little ball-busting wasn't so bad.

When he turned on the lights to the stockroom and saw it was empty, he frowned. The drive over he'd been hoping Tina was going to greet him. He couldn't stop thinking about her, even though he knew doing anything would be like cheating on Alli.

Alli left you, asshole, Jackson thought. He went back to the bar and drank some coffee. Picked a chocolate glazed donut from the box and bit into it.

There was still so much work to be done before he could attempt to get an inspector through the door. He'd start on some of the electrical issues this afternoon. He knew he'd need to spend way too much money to get the building even close to code. While he knew he'd be able to rig a few things and hide even more to pass inspection, they always took a good look at the wiring of an old building like this.

He'd been in construction long enough to know the inspectors and knew a couple of them were easy to get through. A cup of coffee, some small talk about the Yankees or Giants, and he was good to go.

The stockroom door opened and swung slowly, squeaking a little.

Jackson nearly dropped his donut. "Uh... Trevor? That you?"

He knew it wasn't.

The door had finished opening, inches from the wall. The lights were still on but at this angle Jackson couldn't see inside, but there was a shadow.

"Hey... we're closed," Jackson said. He knew it was her and she was calling to him without saying a word. "Tina?"

He heard what could've been a quiet laugh. Jackson put down the donut and coffee and walked to the door, his feet betraying him.

Jackson wanted to run away but he couldn't. Not when he saw Tina, standing in the center of the room with nothing on but a smile.

She turned slowly and bent over, revealing her great ass and long legs.

"Hey, Jackson. I was wondering when you were coming back. Wanna have some fun?"

Jackson nodded dumbly, fighting with his belt and zipper to get rid of his damn jeans.

He glanced back to make sure no one was in the bar area before going back to Tina, who was on all fours on the ground on the tarp again.

"I want you to start really slow but fuck me hard when I tell you, baby." Tina licked her lips. "But first I want to suck your cock."

Jackson went to take a step into the stockroom and stopped. "Why don't we do it against the bar? Even on the bar."

140

Tina sat up on her knees and shook her head. "Right here. Right now. On the floor or nothing. Are you a fag?"

"What? No. Not at all," Jackson said and blushed.

"Then do me." Tina got back down and grinned. "By the hard on trying to get out of your underwear I knew you weren't into dudes. Just fucking with ya. Now fuck me."

Jackson entered and it felt surreal. The lights dimmed. The stockroom had shelves and stock. He could smell beer. Kegs were stacked on either side of the aisle.

He stepped in front of Tina and slid off his underwear.

"When you fuck me, I want you to call me Alli," Tina said and took him in her mouth before he could fully process what she'd said.

· · · **XXX** · · ·

Trevor thought he'd been followed. He'd taken his time, driven through the city and cut back and forth, doubling back.

At least two black SUV's had been spotted in his rearview mirror in the last hour. He was running out of gas and felt like he was running out of time.

He took another glance at the three bulging envelopes on the passenger seat. There might be enough there to buy a new identity, a plane ticket and a new life in another country. He'd always wanted to go to Mexico. Brazil? Somewhere warm with dark-skinned women with big asses.

There was definitely a tail and he couldn't shake it. At least five cars were keeping pace, falling back and catching up in seemingly random patterns he knew were anything but random.

Trevor knew he was wasting time. He'd run out of gas soon, too. All it would take was stopping at a gas station and one of them doing a drive by and making it look like a random gang hit.

I need to get to the building and give Jackson the envelopes, Trevor thought, taking another look at them. All that money he'd never be able to spend. Money he didn't want to have, except his fair share. He wanted to keep working and making cash to help out his bro.

At some point soon, Trevor figured he'd have enough to live and help and he'd walk away from The Family and illegal jobs. Turn his life around. Become a bartender and meet hot women. Have a few beers and laughs and die an old, happy man. He wasn't asking for too much.

Right now, he was only asking to live long enough to say goodbye to Jackson.

Apologize for being a shitty bro. For always getting into trouble and needing Jackson to bail him out. This time he needed to do it himself, or it would be the last time it would matter.

Trevor had visions of cement shoes and a kiss on either cheek before The Family tossed him into the Hudson River, where he'd drown, if the pollution didn't kill him first.

He made a couple of quick and illegal turns down one-way streets the wrong way, knowing this early in the morning these streets weren't likely to be used. He crossed his fingers and hoped so, anyway.

Once he was sure he'd lost them, even for a few minutes, he parked in a loading zone behind a building that hadn't opened for business yet, grabbed the envelopes and ran two blocks down alleys until he reached Jackson's place.

"Yo, bro, you here?" Trevor was out of breath. He'd need to stop smoking if he wanted to be able to run like that anymore.

As if, after today, I'll need to worry about it, Trevor thought. He saw coffee and donuts on the bar, which meant Jackson was here somewhere. "Jackson? You here?"

The door to the stockroom opened and Jackson came out, looking disheveled. His shirt was on backwards.

Trevor laughed despite what was going on in his life. He downed the warm, but not hot, coffee and locked the front door. He started moving past Jackson, who put a hand out and stopped him.

"Where are you going, Trevor?"

"I need to lock the back door. I'm in trouble."

Jackson looked pissed. He shook his head. "The back

door is locked. I just locked it. Stay out of the stockroom."

"Why?"

Jackson put himself between Trevor and the door. "Because I said so. What kind of trouble are you in?"

"The Family." Trevor put up his hands because it looked like Jackson was going to punch him. "I know. I fucked up. Big time. I've been doing deliveries for them for months. Nothing dangerous. They load up my car with stuff and I drop off my car. Go take a walk. Get some coffee. An hour later I come back, and the stuff is gone and there's an envelope of cash for me. Really simple."

"I don't need to ask what stuff means."

Trevor shook his head. "I never looked."

Jackson snorted and began pacing. "You think you were dropping off diapers?"

"No. Drugs. Maybe guns. I dunno," Trevor said. He sighed. "You can yell at me all you want, but there's more to this story."

"They're after you? You stole from them?"

"Nothing like that. The guy I was working for screwed me over. Took the money and the drugs or guns or whatever and set me up for a fall so he could keep it all for himself." Trevor glanced at the door. "But to answer your first question... they are coming for me."

Both men jumped when the knock at the door came.

· · · **XXX** · · ·

"I know what I have to do," Trevor said. He held out the three envelopes to Jackson. "Take them. Hide them for now. Use the money to finish the building."

"No fucking way. We need to escape through the back." Jackson looked at the stockroom door like it was really the last thing he wanted to do.

Trevor shook his head. "If they're in the front knocking, it means they'll be waiting by the back door for us to run out. The only way to get away is hiding upstairs."

"Then let's go." Jackson took a step but saw Trevor wasn't going to budge.

There was another series of knocks at the door, each one louder and quicker.

"I got this, bro." Trevor knew he was bullshitting. He didn't have anything under control. He'd never been more scared in his life, and he'd just fought two mobsters in the dark in his apartment. "Please go and hide. I need to know you're safe. There's no escape for me. I fucked up. Big time. I messed with the wrong people, and they'll keep coming after me. No matter where I go. You know what they'll do? They'll torture you. Break every bone in your body, one at a time, until you tell them where I am."

"Then don't tell me. Just go."

Trevor sighed. "You don't get it. They'll kill you no matter what. Send word to me they've done it. Send a message. Kill everyone I know. I need to deal with this in my own way." He pushed Jackson. "Please, for the love of God, go hide, you stubborn asshole."

· · · **XXX** · · ·

Trevor knew he was fucked if, when he opened the door, one of them shot him in the face. It wasn't a stretch to think it would happen. At this point, they might be done talking.

He'd taken their money and killed a couple of them. There'd be payback.

Instead of opening the door with wide arms and getting attacked, Trevor slipped to the door and unlocked it. No sense in having them kick it down; although, they might anyway.

He ran back across the bar to the door he'd found. "It's open. Come in."

When it opened, six heavily-armed men rushed in and spread out.

Trevor put up his hands. "Hey, guys. I was about to call you. There's been a misunderstanding. It's a funny story."

A member of The Family Trevor knew only as Norcross smiled and stepped forward. "Where's the money?"

Trevor pointed at the door.

"Get it and we'll leave," Norcross said. Trevor knew that was a lie. He'd stay alive only until they got the money back. For good measure, they'd ransack the building and burn it to the ground as a warning not to mess with The Family.

The door was the only reason Trevor had come here, putting Jackson in danger. If this didn't work... *it has to work*, he thought. "I don't have the key. I slipped it under the door. Sorry. I panicked."

Norcross stepped forward and his cronies followed, pacing with him. The circle tightened around Trevor like a noose until Norcross was inches away, smiling. "I don't think you appreciate what's happening. Open the door, by whatever means possible, or we'll use your head to do it."

As soon as Norcross stepped back, a guy on either side grabbed Trevor by the arms.

"I don't have the key. I guess you're going to have to use me as a battering ram, you stupid douchebag bitch," Trevor said.

Norcross looked pissed, which was all the signal the two men needed to hurl Trevor at the door, thinking it would either crack open or crack his skull open.

Instead... he went through it.

Trevor waved, already sweating, knowing what he was doing was madness.

When he stepped back through the door to the coolness of the bar, he wasn't alone.

· · · **XXX** · · ·

The demon dragged himself from the doorway, dripping ash and cinders on the floor.

"Please be careful," Trevor said. "This is my brother's place." He was trying to joke but he was now more scared of this monster he had unleashed than the mobsters.

Had he jumped from the frying pan into the fire?

"What do you wish?" The demon's voice was deep but not 80's horror movie deep. The demon moved his head back and forth, scanning everyone in the room.

145

One of the mobsters turned to run and the demon plucked him as one foot went into the air to move, lifting him to the ceiling.

"No one leaves unless I say you can leave," the demon said. He looked at Trevor. "What do you wish in exchange for these souls?"

"I want no one to be harmed that means anything to me." Trevor glanced at Norcross, visibly shaken. "In fact, I want you to guard over this building. No one with an evil intent can enter because you'll stand guard for eternity."

"And in exchange?"

Trevor pointed. "You get these assholes."

The demon might have laughed or coughed. It was a wicked sound and spit more ash across the floor. "Not good enough."

Norcross smiled.

Trevor's smile faltered. "Then name your price."

"Your soul, as well as anyone who tries to enter who will do harm." The demon still had the man in his hand. He threw him into his suddenly gaping mouth without a sound.

Everyone in the bar took a step or two back.

"Next one to move away gets eaten as well," the demon said. "I will be allowed to stand guard outside the building, keeping it safe. Taking anyone who would do harm. That is my offer."

Trevor knew there was more to it, but he was struggling to find a way out of this bigger mess he'd created. "Fine. I agree." He stared at Norcross. "Would it be possible to let this one go? So, he can warn the rest of The Family what's happened? The money is gone. Destroyed in the hellfire. Coming back will only feed this demon."

The demon nodded its head. "I like that idea. They won't listen and will feed me for weeks."

Norcross looked from the demon to Trevor.

"I'd run before he changes his mind," Trevor said.

Norcross started to move and so did two of his men, who were scooped up in fiery claws and tossed into the demon's maw. The rest were eaten before Norcross left, without looking back.

"This is my brother's place," Trevor said. "Jackson. He is the most important thing to me. Please keep him safe."

"I will." The demon shrunk to about six foot, the fire turning a sickly yellow. "I will become invisible. Patrol the streets and alleys in the area. Rid it of crime. I sense there is enough here to feed me for centuries. Those trapped inside the building, more than mortals, will be left alone. I don't mess with them."

"What are you talking about?"

The demon nodded its head. "It is time."

Trevor took a step forward and closed his eyes as the demon lifted him with both fiery hands.

· · · *XXX* · · ·

Jackson had been hiding upstairs in one of the closets, paralyzed with fear at the noises below.

Then it was silent, and he felt a weight lifted off the building. He took his time going downstairs. Besides a few piles of ash on the floor and some scuff marks, it was empty.

"Jackson... we need to talk," Tina yelled from the stockroom.

He opened the door and couldn't stop staring at Tina, who was dressed once again in her tight jeans and t-shirt.

"Your brother is a great man. He sacrificed himself to keep you safe. To keep us safe. We're now protected. No harm will come to the bar. You'll need to clean out your apartment and move in upstairs." Tina smiled. "I cannot leave the stockroom, but you can visit me nightly."

"Where's Trevor?"

"Gone. The Family won't bother you anymore. Like I said... you're now protected."

"Now what do I do?"

Tina shrugged. "You use the money to finish. You open in his memory. You raise the first glass in Trevor's honor. You close up the doorway he was trying to open. Never try to open it or everything will be ruined. The morning crew will be here shortly. Put them to work. We'll have fun later. Do you love me?"

Trevor nodded. He did. Everything was going to be perfect now.

· · · XXX · · ·

Alli couldn't help herself. She'd been following Jackson's progress through some of his vendors, as well as doing some old fashioned spying. She'd been sitting in her car at the end of the block. She knew tonight was his grand opening and he'd be excited.

Despite her mother's stern warnings, Alli couldn't help it. She wanted to wish him well.

She walked toward the building, a shiver running up and down her spine. Something was still wrong with the place, but she knew one brief conversation with Jackson wouldn't hurt. She'd wish him well, see if the spark was still there, and see what happened.

If Jackson was interested, Alli had a slew of her mother's friends ready to help cleanse the bar and building. There were so many souls trapped. They'd need to be helped to cross over.

One thing at a time. Alli knocked on the front door. The sound was muffled. Odd.

Alli got a strong sense Jackson was in the parking lot in the back of the building. She didn't know where the thought had come from but it made sense. He'd be doing last-minute prep.

As soon as she rounded the corner to the back, she saw the back door open and an older woman wearing jeans and a t-shirt waved at her. "You must be Alli."

"I am," Alli said, confused.

"We've been expecting you. Please, come in."

Alli got to the doorway and felt the intense presence behind her, barring her path.

"I get her first, on the tarp," Tina said.

"No. A deal's a deal. I eat her," the demon standing behind Alli said.

THE LAST TAPROOM ON THE EDGE OF THE WORLD

(IV)

PAUL HAD JUST finished the story when Nolan realized they weren't heading back to the Ocean View Hotel. The thought that he should open the passenger's door and bail prevailed once again. They were going about fifty and, at this speed, he didn't think the fall and tumble across pavement would kill him. He was pretty sure he'd survive. Might land himself in a hospital bed for a day or two, but his confidence level was high. A few broken bones. Some scratches and bumps. But he'd live.

Wouldn't kill me. No way.

And the best part? He'd be away from Paul McDaniel and his stories.

His hand went for the handle. Paul didn't see him, or, if he did, he kept his mouth closed. Maybe he wanted him to do it. Kill himself by throwing himself out of a moving vehicle.

Nolan, at the last second, decided against the potentially suicidal maneuver. He still had a lot to live for. A loving wife. A baby on the way. A job he liked that paid fairly well. He got to travel, live in New York City. It was a cozy life, full of happiness and no regrets. Certainly not worth risking trying to escape from Paul McDaniel's wild ride.

"Where are we going?" Nolan asked, lowering his hand to his side.

"Well, I told you I'd take you back home, but that was a lie."

Nolan pounded the door with his fist.

"Whoa! Easy with the merchandise there, friend. No need to act hateful."

"I went on this ride with you expecting you to show me something that I could use. So far, you've told me three stories I'll never be able to fact-check and you've made me dig up an empty casket in the middle of a goddamn Nor'easter. Tell me—am I supposed to be ecstatic about that?"

"I think I've given you some A-plus material. And I have one more thing to show you."

"Oh, boy. Can't wait. What will it be this time? A palm reader who will tell me when I die? A dead body in the middle of the woods? Oh, I know. I bet it's a New Jersey diner that doesn't serve pork roll."

"Jesus Christ, you're wound tight. Here..."

Paul reached down, under his seat. When his hand resurfaced from the darkness below, it was holding a sixteen ounce can of craft beer. He cracked the top and offered it to Nolan, who looked at him as if the old man had completely lost it.

"Have you lost your goddamn mind?" shouted Nolan. "You can't open a container of alcohol in a moving vehicle! If we get pulled over, we're both going to jail."

"Stop being such a pussy." He continued to hold the can between them. "Take it. Drink it. It'll loosen you up a little. Which might be good for where we're going."

Nolan reluctantly accepted the can. He read the label. *Lost Demon Brewing. Blood-Orange IPA. Satan's Pour* was written in bold white lettering under the brewery's logo, an open door leading into a fiery abyss.

"Been saving that one for a rainy day," Paul said, smiling at himself in the rearview.

"Lost Demon?"

"Yeah, figured I'd resurrect the brand. We plan on launching some new beers next month. What do you think of the label?"

Nolan rotated the can. The label showed a vision of Hell—towers of fire, demons walking across molten rivers, thrones made of human skulls—and Nolan felt his skin move.

"Drink it," Paul urged.

"No."

"Drink it." This time he spoke with venom. When Nolan didn't react, Paul reached under the seat again.

When his hand returned from the darkness, Nolan nearly jumped through the window. "What the fuck, man!" He found himself staring down the barrel of a .45.

"I said drink the goddamn beer," Paul said, the gun in his hand unwavering. "Or so help me God, I'll blow your fucking brains out all over the goddamn place. And I don't want to do that because of the mess. Understand?"

Nolan's hand trembled so much that a splash of beer danced up from the mouth of the can, spilled over the rim.

"Drink it!"

Nolan flinched. He reached for the door, pulled the lever, and braced himself for his meeting with the unforgiving pavement.

But the door didn't open.

"Don't be a fool," Paul said. "You're not going anywhere. Now, drink the goddamn beer or kiss your goddamn life good-fucking-bye."

Slowly, Nolan brought the can to his mouth. He sipped the blood-orange IPA. It was quite good, fruity and hoppy. He took another sip, and not because Paul McDaniel and his gun told him to, but because he actually enjoyed the flavor, the bold combination of orange and grapefruit and the bitter bite of the hops.

"Taste good?" Paul asked.

"Yes. Very."

"Hm. Maybe we're ready to launch after all."

"We? Who else is involved?"

Paul took his eyes off the empty road and stared at him. Then, he lowered his gun before stashing it on the dashboard behind the steering wheel, close enough in case he had to use it again. Nolan decided it was best not to provoke that scenario and to listen to everything the man told him to do. At least that way he might make it through this alive.

"Don't worry about it," Paul told him. With his eyes back on the wet road, he nodded. "We're almost there."

The wipers cleared away the obscured view outside. Paul turned the car down another dark street, this one stocked with empty buildings and rundown establishments. Stores that used to be thriving businesses now sat in ruin, casualties of the cancerous economy and hard times had by all. In the near distance, at the end of the road, Nolan finally saw where Paul was taking him.

Bayberry Bluff.

Nolan had never felt so terrified in all his life.

· · · **XXX** · · ·

Paul stabbed Nolan in the back with the barrel of his .45, pushing him along. Nolan had dragged his feet since they had left the car. He didn't want to go anywhere near Bayberry Bluff. Not because of the stories he'd been told, but because the building had been abandoned since Jackson tried reopening the brewery in the nineties. Who knew what was inside? Rats, bums.

Monsters.

Ghosts.

Demons.

No, Nolan knew better than that. Even though he'd investigated the paranormal his entire adult life, the stories always ended the same—never enough proof or corroboration to prove anything. Monsters and demons were just figments of people's imaginations, mirages that hid the truth behind it all. Excuses for things that sometimes had no obvious explanation. Nothing more than stories, lies people told each other to entertain.

Nolan felt weird when Paul walked him inside the abandoned facility, like he'd stepped through a portal into another world. Huge cracks zigged and zagged up the walls, coupled with an excessive amount of graffiti. He couldn't tell what the colorful collection of spray paint was supposed to embody, but he figured they were gang symbols and coded messages not meant for him. The tiled floor was also cracked, almost every single tile chipped or broken in some obscene way. Piles of trash, splintered lumber and leftover construction materials occupied the corners. Some garbage spilled over to common walking areas, making it impossible for them to shuffle about without paying attention to each step. The last thing Nolan wanted was a rusty nail through his foot. There was so much dust in the place it seemed like they were walking in a fog. The only light was provided by the pre-dawn glow that infiltrated the windows.

He tried to run through the night's events, figure out why Paul had brought him here. He didn't buy into his story, the whole "I want to help you with your book" angle. There had to be something else, something he'd missed.

What does he want with me?

And furthermore, why was he holding a gun to his back? It didn't add up. Paul McDaniel, who'd seemed like a fairly nice guy, if a little quirky, had turned into quite the asshole.

He should have known when he saw that vision back at the hotel, the one of the bloodied girl. He still didn't believe what he'd seen was real, but maybe it had been his mind's way of warning him. Telling him to get the hell out of there.

He should have listened.

Just steady the course. Get out of this alive. And then sue this motherfucker for all he's worth.

Paul walked him into the next room. What was left of the bar remained in the corner. Dust blanketed the countertop. Cobwebs infested the ceiling. An old television, bulky and twenty times the size of a modern flat screen, rested on the shelf above the bar. Someone had taken a bat to its face, smashed in the screen. A mess of wires hung out of it, spools of electric noodles dangling freely. Nolan expected his allergies to kick in, his nose to fill with garbage and for the sneezing attacks to overcome him. Somehow, his body managed to keep it together.

"Head to the back. See that door?"

Nolan faced the door his captor referenced. It was

closed, and, for some reason, not ridden with dust and dirt and grime like the rest of the derelict facility.

"You know in 1926, back when this was a prison for the criminally insane, they tested electroshock therapy on patients back there. Just beyond that door. Rumors have it they killed a few. Cranked the machine up too high, scrambled their brains. Not that their brains weren't already scrambled, if you know what I mean."

Nolan had come across the same rumors while researching the place. There was no validity to these claims. Just rumors. Conjecture. There was evidence that such experimental procedures had taken place, but that they had resulted in deaths was never confirmed.

"A whole slew of crazies were executed. Some believe it was because they were incurable. Cancers to society. They were killed because the facility had no further use for them. They couldn't cure them, couldn't learn from them, so what was the alternative? Let them live out their days, taking up space for those who could benefit from treatments? No, they couldn't have that. So, the insane, the really bad ones, they killed. *Murdered.*"

"I don't believe you."

"Believe me or don't," Paul said, and Nolan could picture him shrugging. "I don't give a shit."

"Why did you bring me here?"

"To show you the truth, of course. So, you can write about it in your fancy little book. I hope it makes millions. I hope Netflix does a docu-drama on it. That would be *real* nice."

The way Paul laughed suggested he didn't truly wish those things. In fact, Nolan got the sense he didn't want him to write his book at all.

"You're lying."

"Am I?"

The gun pressed harder against his spine.

"You don't want me to write about Bayberry Bluff. About Lost Demon Brewing. That's what this is all about, isn't it?"

Silence. No words. Somewhere in the building, a board creaked. He swore he heard a pipe groan.

"You brought me here to kill me."

Nolan turned to him. Paul didn't stop him. He let them face each other, keeping the gun aimed ahead, finger on the trigger.

"That's it, isn't it? I told you about the book, my plans on bringing its history to the masses, and you thought that meeting with me, taking me on this trip down memory lane so to speak, would be the perfect opportunity to stop me."

"It's nothing personal, Mr. Nolan. We just can't have the truth about this place out there. It wouldn't do well."

Nolan sneered. "You son of a bitch. I should have known."

Paul yawned. "Listen, friend. It's a messed-up world we live in. It can be harsh sometimes."

"You'll never get away with it. My wife... she'll look for me. She knows where I was tonight, and she'll ask questions. So will the police. Especially if there's a bullet hole in me."

That smile again, sinister and savage. "Who said anything about a bullet hole? I was thinking suicide. See, come morning, my handyman will call the police, tell them a man hung himself in that old brewery. He'll be here at the crack of dawn to start fixing up the place, and not a second sooner. You wouldn't imagine the things that happen come nightfall. In fact, we probably shouldn't stick around too long." He checked his watch. "We're close enough to morning. Maybe it won't matter."

"Fix it up? You're going to fix it up?"

"I think it's a great spot to open a new brewery. The renovations shouldn't take long, not once we get a demo crew in here to clean out the joint."

Nolan shook his head. "Why the theatrics? Why take me to the cemetery? Tell me the stories?"

Paul cocked his head back and laughed. "Oh, man. You're right. Well, truth is, I didn't know if Dusty's grave would be empty or not. But I suspected. See, even in death, the fucker couldn't stay away from this place." He nodded to the door.

Nolan rotated toward the far wall, where the demon door stood looking clean, in pristine condition, as if it had just been installed earlier that night. "Are you trying to tell me that Dusty rose from the grave just to walk through that door?"

"I'm saying there're a great many possibilities. But yes, I had to know what had become of my old friend. I had to know what I was dealing with. This place will need to be cleansed in more ways than one. Can't have all the same mistakes happening all over again."

Nolan rubbed his eyes. He felt unusually tired. The road beer was clearly having its effect on him. "Madness."

"Oh yes. That word again."

"The stories. Why tell me if you just planned on killing me?"

"Stories pass the time. Plus, I think it's important to know what you died for. You wanted your book? Well, you got it. Shame you won't live long enough to write it."

"That's what you think."

Nolan turned and sped toward the door. He reached the handle in almost no time at all. He'd expected Paul to shoot him, but he knew the bastard couldn't risk it. A body being discovered in a building with his name attached to it, one riddled with bullet holes—that would raise one too many questions. He wasn't going to shoot him. Never planned on it.

Nolan turned the doorknob, then glanced over his shoulder, back at Paul. "I'll do it. I'll open it. I'll let the demons out." He hoped to God Paul believed in the nonsense he'd told him that night. If he did, then maybe he'd be scared, frightened to release whatever lived on the other side. But if he didn't believe... if he thought the stories were bullshit... then Nolan had no more tricks up his sleeve.

I'm not gonna die like this.

Paul was smiling. Behind him, Nolan saw the bloodied girl again. She shook her head "no." Another warning. She was naked, every inch of flesh showered in red. No skin. Just blood. Animated, she whipped her head back and forth.

Don't do it, he almost heard her say. *Don't you dare.*

"You gonna let me go now, McDaniel?" Nolan asked. "Huh?"

No answer. Paul stood there, watching on. His eyes slimmed.

"Answer me!"

"You know I can't let you live," Paul told him. "Not when so much is at stake. I thought, after telling you the history of this place, you'd understand."

"Fuck you, asshole!"

Nolan ripped open the door. A void, infinitely dark and endless, greeted him. There was nothing there except an opaque wall. He waited for his eyes to adjust, to show him details, a deeper level of the lair he'd just revealed... but there was nothing. A black world beyond the door, cold and lifeless.

"What were you expecting?" Paul asked. "Hellfire and brimstone? A horde of demons?"

A picture of the Lost Demon Brewing can flashed in his mind, the logo. Hellfire. Brimstone. It had been there. But not here. Here, only darkness.

Nolan felt a presence in the dark, some unknown entity making its rounds. When he turned back to Paul, he felt a chill brush against his neck, gentle as a feather. There was something behind him all right, lurking about the dark, biding its time, waiting for the opportunity to strike. He couldn't look. Didn't dare to.

"What's... what's down there?"

Paul chuckled, his smirk widening. The bloodied woman behind him had vanished, fled once the doorway had been opened. Nolan could still hear her warning echoing through his thoughts. Those words never left him.

Don't do it.

Don't do it.

DON'T DO IT.

Paul took a deep breath. "Some doors should never be opened, friend."

Two arms, covered in an ashen, powdery substance, cracked and split like blistered earth, reached out from the dark chasm and grabbed hold of Nolan around his waist. His breath was immediately squeezed from his chest. He felt his ribs crack inward, puncturing his lungs. Pain settled in, covering him from head to toe. There was a split second when he tried to escape, use all the strength he had to break free. But that moment came and went in a blink. Next, he was stolen from the room, the dark of the mystery room swallowing him whole.

He fell.

The luminance from the doorway shrank, became nothing but a small square light. Then it became nothing. All dark, all the time.

Then he felt hands all over him. Groping him. Feeling him. *Digging* into him. He heard people moaning; the language of the dead. The mentally ill. Their ghosts. They surrounded him. Down there, in the dark, they ripped him apart.

Feasted on his soul.

Soon the pain stopped.

And all he saw and felt was perpetual darkness.

$$\cdots XXX \cdots$$

Outside, Paul walked to his car, which was parked along the curb. Another vehicle approached, stopped right behind his sedan. Sylvester, the bartender, got out. It had stopped raining and the crack of dawn was beginning to wedge its way over the horizon. Purple light spilled across the street, forming shadows on the long row of empty, cracked buildings.

"Where's the handyman?" Paul asked. "He's late."

"He'll be here soon," Sylvester said, as if he weren't sure. "Told him six."

"Well, if he's not here by six-oh-five, fire his ass. Hire someone else. We need this shit-hole cleaned up ASAP."

"Okay, boss."

"We're opening next month. I don't care what the builders tell us—it will be done."

"You got it, boss."

"The writer's body is inside. Hanging most likely. I mean, shit, I hope so. Either way, make sure the handyman makes the call to 911. That's important. Got it?"

"Yes, boss."

"Repeat it, you imbecile."

"Handyman phones the police."

"Close enough."

Paul turned to his car, spotted a figure across the street. The naked woman covered in blood. The woman who'd been following him for the last two weeks. Next to her, Dusty the coach. They stared him on, challenging him. Begging him to make the next move. Or maybe... just maybe they were warning him. Telling him to stop.

He'd never listen.

"The Family is fronting us the money," Paul told Sylvester. "That means no screw-ups. You hear?"

"Yes, boss."

"Good. Because they'll kill us. No question. We're in deep now. Too deep." Paul blinked and his friends across the street were gone. Tired, beyond exhausted, he cleared his lungs with a deep sigh. "I need a fucking drink."

THE HAUNTED BREWERY

THE LAST TAPROOM ON THE EDGE OF THE WORLD
by Tim Meyer

NO FORTUNATE SON
by Chuck Buda

HAVE A DRINK ON ME
by Frank Edler

ALTERNATIVE
by Armand Rosamilia

SPECIAL THANKS

The world is a better place thanks to the people who toil each day to craft the best-tasting beer one can enjoy.

We owe our sincerest gratitude to some special folks who create delicious craft beers and invite us into their hospitable breweries to spend quality time with our fans.

We love these breweries and highly recommend all their creations!

Angry Erik Brewing – www.angryerik.com
Hampton Township, NJ

Belford Brewing Company – www.belfordbrewing.com
Belford, NJ

Jughandle Brewing Company – www.jughandlebrewing.com
Tinton Falls, NJ

Spellbound Brewing – www.spellboundbrewing.com
Mt. Holly, NJ

For those who have visited us in these fine establishments, you already know how wonderful these breweries are.

For those who couldn't join us, you should go out of your way to visit these breweries and sample their wonderful creations. Tell them the Beers N Fears fellas sent you!

Cheers!

ABOUT THE AUTHORS

CHUCK BUDA - Chuck Buda explores the darkest aspects of the human condition. Then he captures its essence for fictional use. He writes during the day and wanders aimlessly all night...alone. Join his mailing list for free stories and things of horrifying weirdness: https://www.chuckbuda.com

FRANK EDLER - Frank J. Edler resides in New Jersey where he attempts to write. He is the author of SCATTERBRAIN, BRATS IN HELL, DEATH GETS A BOOK and SCARED SILLY. He is the co-author of the SHOCKER trilogy. His work walks the fine line between horror, humor and weird fiction. When he is not writing, Frank is host of Bizzong! The Bizarre and Weird Fiction Podcast.

TIM MEYER - Tim Meyer dwells in a dark cave near the Jersey Shore. He's an author, husband, father, podcast host, blogger, coffee connoisseur, beer enthusiast, and explorer of worlds. He writes horror, mysteries, science fiction, and thrillers, although he prefers to blur genres and let the stories fall where they may. You can follow Tim at https://timmeyerwrites.com OR like his Facebook page here: www.facebook.com/authortimmeyer

ARMAND ROSAMILIA - Armand Rosamilia is a New Jersey boy currently living in sunny Florida, where he writes when he's not sleeping. He's happily married to a woman who helps his career and is supportive, which is all he ever wanted in life... He's written over 150 stories that are currently available, including horror, zombies, contemporary fiction, thrillers and more. His goal is to write a good story and not worry about genre labels.

You can find him at http://armandrosamilia.com for not only his latest releases but interviews and guest posts with other authors he likes!